DEATH FROM ABOVE

Whoop-whoop-whoop. The 'copter sped above the Texas prairie. All their instructions ran back through Rosie's head. The barracks would be full of hardcore security guards. Hard men, they were as dangerous as they came. Trying to rescue Cowboy from this stronghold might be more than even he *and* Applebaum could handle!

Applebaum leaned out the chopper door and fired the disposable LAWs in rapid sequence. One, two . . . three . . . four, five. The rockets' plastic firing tubes looked like toys. When the 'copter veered and Rosie saw the destruction he thought *some toys.* Flames roared from what had been, ten seconds before, the mercs' barracks. Rosie could see the small figures standing still and then on some command, running like all hell had broken loose. *Like Satan himself when he sees Jesus coming,* Rosie mused. *Jesus in the air, with sworded angels in cammie!*

OTHER BOOKS IN THE BLACK BERETS SERIES:

LOUISIANA FIRESTORM

Mike McCray

A DELL BOOK

Published by
Dell Publishing Co., Inc.
1 Dag Hammarskjold Plaza
New York, New York 10017

Dell ® TM 681510, Dell Publishing Co., Inc.

ISBN: 0-440-14999-1

Printed in the United States of America
First printing—March 1985

DD

I like a look of Agony,
Because I know it's true—
Men do not sham Convulsion
Nor simulate, a Throe—

The Eyes glaze once—and that is Death—
Impossible to feign
The Beads upon the Forehead
By homely Anguish strung.

—Emily Dickinson

For V K McCarty

1

"It would have to be a place like this."

Billy Leaps Beeker wasn't the kind of man who enjoyed the high polish, high plastic of the New Orleans hotel-restaurant he was sitting in. He scowled at the waiters and made no effort to disguise his discomfort. He was a big man, six-foot-one of hard muscle, the kind that showed in the neck where the mass of flesh was drawn into tight rope-like sinew. He was tanned, but the darkness of his skin wasn't just exposure to the sun. He was half Cherokee. His dislike for this fancy restaurant rose principally out of his adamant refusal to give up that part of himself. The non-Cherokee part of him showed through plainly enough, though, in his blue eyes. Eyes that came from his mother.

The sixteen-year-old boy who sat across the table wasn't going to argue with Beeker. Not just because the big ex-Marine was his adopted father, but also because Tsali was mute, had been since birth. The boy had the same warm brown skin as Beeker, but not the blue eyes. Tsali was a full-blooded Cherokee, a dwindling breed.

He was part of another vanishing breed as well. A son who respected, even revered, his father. Billy Leaps had saved the kid's life less than a year earlier. Redneck hunters thought they had caught themselves some easy fun in the person of the mute Indian boy. Instead they had caught a few bullets, enough to tamp them six feet under in a pine forest near Shreveport, close to where Billy Leaps and Tsali now lived with the rest of the men. Tsali had never forgotten the debt he owed his old man. Even the fact he'd repaid the favor with some precocious killings of his own while he defended his father's farm from the team's enemies hadn't wiped out the other obligations he owed the big man. Billy Leaps hadn't just saved Tsali's life, he'd given the boy an entirely new existence. One with friends and meaning, discipline and rewards, a tradition to follow, even a room of his own. He'd never had any of that.

So Tsali wasn't even about to use sign language to contradict Beeker. He just looked out the floor-to-ceiling picture window that framed a view of the Mississippi. He watched with unflagging interest the intricate movements of the flotilla of ships in this, one of America's busiest harbors.

The third person at the table wasn't going to let Beeker off so easy. She smiled knowingly. When Delilah smiled waiters stopped moving in the middle of the floor. They looked at her with undisguised lust. She had that effect on men. All men. Even Beeker let his scowl go. Delilah was almost the only woman to get to the Cherokee in the last decade—since Vietnam. It disturbed him, upset him to no end. Every time he came near her his shell of emotional invulnerability shattered like a glass bell beneath the solid stroke of a hammer. His need for a woman roared to the surface. Before Delilah, he could go months without noticing it. But when he saw Delilah's breasts, perfect cream-colored mounds that seemed impossible to contain in any kind of clothing, or when he studied those hips of hers, firm and fleshy below a tight waist, then . . .

Delilah got to Beeker. Even though Beeker had gotten to Delilah just a couple of hours ago in her hotel room.

Maybe she felt that gave her the right to rib him now. Though, really, she didn't need much of an excuse. Delilah was always ready to prod the tough exterior that Beeker showed the world. "It seems to me that this is just the right sort of place for a land baron to dine. After all, now that you've bought *another* hundred acres of land it seems to me you must be climbing up the list of Louisiana's biggest landowners."

"Hundred and ninety-two acres," growled Beeker. "That's nothing in a state like this."

"You could afford more."

He shook his head. He didn't have to explain to her. He wasn't interested in buying land for investment. He'd never think of sinking any of his substantial wealth into land that was distant from his home. He owned a farm near Shreveport, and when any land that was contiguous to his holdings came up, he purchased it. Plot by plot and field by field he was increasing the size of the farm, that was all. He frowned. He wasn't a goddamn developer.

"Hundred and ninety-two acres is room enough for five men—" said Beeker.

"Six men," corrected Delilah with a smile for Tsali.

There were four more adults who lived on Beeker's farm, the other four who had fought with him in Vietnam—the other four who had tried to fit back into an American society that not only didn't honor them, Beeker thought, but hated them, reviled them, even persecuted them. The "good citizens" and politicians of America had shoved them out to fight in Asia. Now they were doing their damnedest to keep that same door shut against them. The "good citizens" and hypocritical politicians, Beeker thought, wanted to exclude the thousands of broken, burnt, battered men who told a single story: *We fought the war that wasn't meant to be won. We who died filled your cemeteries, and we who survived give business to the guys who sew straitjackets.*

The five of them—the Black Berets—had tried to reintegrate themselves into America. Beeker had actually married—he made that mistake twice before reverting to a committed bachelorhood. He'd taught in a private school in Shreveport, a second-rate boys' military school where the little snots under his tutelage could have used a swift kick in the ass with a military boot every hour on the hour. And five months in boot camp after that.

The other Black Berets had tried too. There was Harry the Greek. Actually it was Haralambos Georgeos Papathanessiou, but who could pronounce that? Harry seemed to have left his soul in Vietnam. What was left of him stood propped up behind a bar in Chicago. All Beeker had to do was tell Harry they were getting back together and the Greek wadded up his apron and slammed it down on the counter. He wasn't the guy to spend the rest of his life

9

snapping open Pabsts for the local steelworkers. Harry'd seen too much in Vietnam. If you looked at the expression in his eyes, you might think he was seeing it still.

Rosie—big, black Roosevelt Boone—had at least got a job that used his skills. Beeker had found him peeling the skin off cadavers in the basement of a Newark hospital. The salvaged skin was used as bandages for burn victims. But few people were ready to wind human bandages as a full-time job—and it wasn't just the tedium that discouraged them. Rosie didn't mind it. Rosie had done the same thing with living men in 'Nam. Doing it with stiffs was easy. But "easy" wasn't something that was going to make Rosie happy. Being back with the Black Berets was the only thing that could do that. When Rosie looked up and saw Beeker standing in that doorway, he wiped off his scalpel and was ready to take off.

Marty Applebaum was ready to rejoin the team as well—too ready. Marty blew up buildings for a living. Marty had the finesse with a stick of dynamite that Minnesota Fats had with a cue stick. Beeker knew the regrouped Black Berets had to have that skill— trouble was, Marty Applebaum came along with it. He had a wheezy face framed in scraggly pale-blond hair. He had bad sinuses and his voice sounded worse. He drove everybody but Harry up the wall. Sometimes Harry could even persuade Marty to shut up. But only sometimes.

They needed Cowboy too. They had to have a flyer. Cowboy was one of the best. His father had been one of the original old barn-stormers. Cowboy had grown up spending more time in the air than on the ground. After the Air Force gave him jet training, Cowboy could fly anything. Cowboy could take a junked Volkswagen, a surfboard, and a ceiling fan, put the whole thing together and get it in the air in five minutes—and that was at night. Under fire.

Cowboy could *fly*. But the idea didn't take the scowl off Beeker's face. Cowboy could fly all right, on just about any chemical that could be sold on the street. Damn lunatic just never seemed to understand that you can't mix fighting with drugs, Beeker thought. But for Cowboy cocaine was the only way to go. When they were in the field, Beeker kept a lid on the drug use. But the Cherokee knew that every time he turned his back . . .

He'd better not be doing it with Tsali. Beeker looked over at his adopted son. Adopted was such a wrong-headed and inadequate word to describe their relationship. Hell, Beeker couldn't remember how life was lived before he rescued the boy and brought him into his house. The Cherokee bond was so strong between them that they were much closer than most fathers and sons lucky enough to share the biological bond. Beeker was utterly bound to Tsali—he was actually aching at this moment. It wasn't just the idea of Cowboy getting the kid on drugs—Tsali wouldn't fall in with that. As much as Beeker complained about Cowboy's attempts to lead the boy astray, Beeker knew that the fancy-acting Cowboy was a necessary counterbalance to Beeker's own drive. If Beeker was Tsali's adoptive father, then Cowboy was the kid's adoptive big brother. After all, it was Cowboy who got the kid laid for the first time—just the sort of thing big brothers are good at, Beeker thought, and fathers aren't . . .

But Beeker's ache came because of their secondary purpose in coming to New Orleans. Tsali was going to be left there. At a big fancy private military academy. Damn, what the boy sure didn't need was a bunch of assholes filling him with bullshit. The real military was bad enough when it came to bullshit. And this was *fake* military. The farm was the boy's home, Beeker thought, the place where Tsali could learn everything he needed to know to be a man. He could teach the boy marksmanship, Cowboy flying, Harry—

"It's good for him to spend some time with boys his own age." Delilah seemed to be reading Beeker's mind. That, or else she'd noticed the way his fists were bunching up under the table. They always did when Beeker got angry and couldn't hit anybody. Tsali was going away—and there wasn't anybody he could hit. Not the boy—he was being told what to do. Not himself—he had made the final decision. Not Delilah—she had only chosen the school once the decision had been made. It was lucky there wasn't a waiter nearby at that moment.

"He can't grow up with just the five of you," Delilah went on.

"Why not?" demanded Beeker.

"No reason, I suppose," Delilah said, "as long as you're prepared to consider Marty Applebaum as a role model for an impressionable Cherokee youth. . . ."

She smiled at Tsali, to let him in on the joke. But it wasn't a joke to Beeker. He saw real reason in her jibe at Marty. When it came down to it, Beeker *wasn't* prepared to accept Marty as a role model for his boy. Or Rosie, either, for that matter. Rosie had a little core of violence in him, and inside that core of violence was an even harder little core of cruelty. There was a gentler side beneath all that, but getting to that took more than any boy could have managed.

Tsali just looked out the window. He heard everything that was said, but he'd heard it all before. Nothing in his movements, nothing in his eyes betrayed the emotion he felt that moment. The boy was desolate at the thought of leaving his father's farm.

How many times had he been thrown out of a place before? More than he could count. Tsali had been a ward of the State of Louisiana for as long as he could remember—almost since birth. Full-blooded Indian orphans with noticeable disabilities are given short shrift by the state welfare department. Foster homes. Juvenile centers. Orphanages run by various religious denominations. In one place he was judged retarded. In another a delinquent. An underachiever. A malcontent. A misfit.

No one wrote on the boy's record: *Starved for affection. Would benefit from strong guidance. Requires stability to overcome handicap.*

At last he'd found all that. Affection. Guidance. Stability.

Now he had to employ every ounce of his courage to believe that he wasn't losing it. That Billy Leaps Beeker wasn't just farming him out as he had been farmed twenty times before. He knew it wasn't so. He knew his father hated to let him go. He knew his father loved him. He knew the other men would miss him.

He knew he was leaving the one true home he had ever known. This time, however, he knew why. He was being sent away because his father felt he should be educated. So he'd prove himself for his father. He'd show his father he could stand on his own. He'd show Billy Leaps Beeker everything but his tears.

Tsali looked down at his plate, and pressed his teeth into his lip to keep it from trembling. His gaze slipped past his watch, and he looked up suddenly. He touched his father's arm, and pointed at the time.

"Eight twenty-eight," said Beeker, interrupting his argument with Delilah.

Delilah and Beeker were at once silent. Three pairs of eyes turned to face the window. Beyond the bright white lights of the dock the night was clear. A three-quarter moon reflected off the wide river. On the far side of the river, the levee was an undulating ribbon of black. Ships moved smoothly up and down the Mississippi. Their markings were a vocabulary of world politics. A tanker from Japan. A freighter from Norway. Tsali searched out their flags and used them as a little quiz on his self-study of world geography. The ships were beautiful. Quiet and silent behind the big glass windows, with tiny white lights strung from their—

B-BA-BARRROOOOOM!

The entire vista was suddenly illuminated by an enormous cloud of orange and red flame.

Three explosions, exactly timed, had blown apart the freighter that Tsali had identified as Norwegian. Large furled shards of iron and plastic and burning wood flew high into the air and plunged down again into the murky waters of the river.

Smaller explosions continued, as inflammable stores on the boat were ignited.

The boat, engulfed in black roiling smoke, was invisible.

The restaurant was turned into pandemonium. Women screamed. Men overturned their tables. Waiters threw down their trays. Everyone rushed to the windows. One woman continued to scream hysterically. The maitre d' was frantically attempting to dial a number on his desk telephone, but his fingers wouldn't work right. He was about to call out to one of the waiters to help him when he suddenly caught sight of the trio in the corner of the restaurant, right by the window. He stopped dead and stared at them in his surprise.

13

Outside all was burning destruction and death. The trio, whose view of the carnage was the best in the restaurant, appeared completely unperturbed. The woman sipped at her drink. The man stared placidly out the window, and now and then checked his watch. The boy was buttering a slice of bread.

The maitre d' staggered over. "You—" he began, but stopped. He's just seen two bodies, or half-bodies, floating on the water near the wreckage of the boat. "Don't you know—" he gasped again.

Delilah held up her glass.

"When you get a chance," she said, "we'd like another round, please."

2

Fire engines had arrived outside on the dock. Police cars. Ambulances. Eyewitness news teams. Gawkers. The black smoke had cleared, and from the restaurant window it was possible to see the blackened hulk burning sullenly in the oil-slicked Mississippi water. The river teemed with rescue craft like small scavenging beetles around a much larger animal whose death throes hadn't quite subsided.

Delilah and Beeker had to talk louder because of the noise beyond the plate-glass window. They were back on the subject of the land Beeker had purchased. He was complaining again about the deal he'd completed the previous week.

"Damn," he said. "They really pulled one on me."

"I told you," said Delilah, sipping her second drink, "you should have checked with me. I could have told you the situation."

"You'd think it'd be easy," said Beeker with disgust. "There's land and somebody owns it. They want to sell it so you make an offer. They accept the offer, you pay good money, you own the land." From the way he spoke, it was obvious something had gone amiss in this latest transaction.

"I looked at the contract," said Delilah. "The right-of-way option was spelled out quite plainly."

"The man didn't *tell* me—"

"When did you all of a sudden start trusting white men?" Delilah asked. "I thought they were all liars and cheats when it came to dealing with Indians."

"They are," said Beeker.

"Then why didn't you read the contract carefully? All you saw was a hundred acres of pine barrens abutting your property, and you thought, 'All right, here's a hundred more acres I can put between me and the rest of civilization.' And when it came up for sale, you snapped it up—without a second thought. You—"

He interrupted her, speaking in a low rasping growl, an intense anger that wasn't characteristic of him. "Goddamned pipeline right down the middle of my farm. . . ."

"It's not down the middle," Delilah pointed out. "It will pass over the farthest corner of the new acreage. *Maybe* you'll hear the workmen during the day—but that would have happened whether you bought the land or not."

"Goddamned thing's not even gonna be sunk," snarled Beeker, piling injury on injury. "Gonna sit there on the fucking ground and one day somebody's gonna come along and bomb it, and there goes me, and there goes Tsali, and there goes our home, blown to heaven and back down to hell again, and you want me not to get upset? Listen, lady, we're—"

"Marty!" Delilah sang out in relief. She was glad that Beeker's ravings—which she'd heard for the past thirty-six hours, endlessly repeated—would be cut short.

Marty Applebaum had just come into the restaurant, and his face glowed with a proud blush when he heard his name called. He liked to hear his name called in public places—especially by beautiful women. It was just too bad that the restaurant was nearly empty, with everyone outside watching the activity around the exploded ship.

"I'm with them," he said loudly to the maitre d', who had come up to him. "Hiya, Del. Kid." He playfully punched Tsali's upper arm. The boy's biceps had been painfully thin not long ago, but they were filling out with the good food and heavy exercise that came with his adoption papers. The mute boy smiled up at Marty, who was still speaking loudly: "Beak—wasn't it great, man? Wasn't it fantastic? Fan-*fucking*-tastic?" Marty clenched his fists and raised them into the air over his head.

"You used too much," complained Beeker. "Nearly blew this

damned window in." He rapped his knuckles against the plate glass.

"Hey look, Beak," said Marty, blushing with the reprimand, and determined to defend himself, "hey look, you didn't tell me to blow that fucker up, you told me to *demolish* it, and that's what I did. Hey Del, you saw it, didn't you?"

Delilah nodded. Marty took one of the empty chairs at the table. Putting both elbows on the table, he leaned far forward.

"Tsali?" he asked.

Tsali nodded.

"Right," said Marty. "Blew that fucker out of the water. One stick more and it would have done a belly flop. I knew what I was doing. You want that ship crippled you get your five waiters out of this goddamned restaurant and have 'em go down on their coffee break. They'll cripple that ship. But you want it *destroyed*, man, you give the job to an artist. I'm an artist, Beak. I'm not a pansy waiter on a coffee break." He turned and looked over his shoulder. "Man," he whispered, in awe of himself, "I *discouraged* that goddamn tin turd."

"Where's Harry?" Beeker wanted to know.

"Cleaning up," said Marty. "He'll be down in a minute."

"Have any trouble with the crew?" Beeker asked.

"Harry picked off a couple of guys. See, Harry was gonna hold back, but I said to him, 'Shit, we're gonna blow 'em up in five minutes.' So after that he didn't hold back."

Marty grinned at Tsali.

"Sometimes," he said, as if he were imparting a valuable lesson to the boy, "a man's just gotta let go."

Delilah called over a waiter and asked him if he would bring them another chair, for a fifth friend who would be joining them shortly. The waiter, who had been desperately trying to overhear their conversation, complied instantly. By the time he got back to the table, Harry the Greek had appeared in the doorway of the dining room. The maitre d' knew instantly what party this great hairy man was with, and simply nodded with a nervous politeness.

Harry came over and sat down, nodding to Delilah, winking solemnly at Tsali.

"Harry," whined Marty, "you know what Beak said? Beak said I used too much shit, that's what he said."

Harry just raised his eyebrows and shrugged. Then after a moment, he said to Billy Leaps: "Marty did a pretty good job out there."

"I know," said Beeker. "Marty, the job was fine. Just right. I jumped on you and I shouldn't have."

"Hey man," grinned Marty, feverishly relieved to be back in Beeker's good graces again. "Hey man, it *might* have been too much shit, but I really don't think it was, I really don't think it was."

"Did you check the cargo?" Delilah asked.

Harry discreetly patted the pocket of his trousers. "Brought you a sample." Then he grinned—and Harry hardly ever smiled. "Poor old Cowboy."

"You never saw so much coke in your life, Billy Leaps," Marty whistled. "I *know* why you left Cowboy at home. Cowboy would have gone down there with a vacuum hose attached to his head, and he wouldn't have come out till Judgment Day."

"And the crew?" Delilah went on. She was actually taking notes in a little pad she had drawn from somewhere. "They were all on board?"

Marty sobered just a little. He realized that they were now submitting a report.

"All on board," said Harry. "Except for the two that came off this afternoon."

Delilah smiled. "I took care of those two," she said with a satisfied smile.

Marty broke into laughter. "You didn't give 'em half a chance, did you, Del?"

Delilah didn't reply. "Anyone on board besides the crew? I had a report—"

"Three girls," said Harry. "Maybe more. Looked South American."

"Sure *is* a good thing we didn't bring Cowboy," Marty crowed. "A boat full of cocaine and South American women—that's Cowboy's definition of died-and-gone-to-heaven."

"Too bad about those women," said Delilah, and something in her eyes suggested that she meant it. "But they were in the game. That ship was to be the first major unloading of cocaine in the New Orleans port. The Colombians were testing the waters. Marty—many thanks. I think you helped us to heat up those waters a little. I think the Colombians will be sticking to Florida for a while. . . ."

3

He kept on forgetting what his name was. Durwood? No, not Durwood. *Sher*wood! That was it. Sherwood . . . Sherwood . . . Thatcher? No, that was the bitch in England. Sherwood . . . Hatcher! Yeah! He was Sherwood Hatcher.

Most men who couldn't even remember their own names would be drunk out of their minds, or psychotic. But it was more understandable for Cowboy to forget the label his parents had slapped on him. *Sherwood Hatcher, not such a bad name,* he thought, and it wasn't. But hardly anyone ever called him that. He was Cowboy. Just plain Cowboy. *Should go to a judge and get the fucker changed,* Cowboy thought. *Just plain old Cowboy.*

That was one of a jumble of thoughts that Cowboy was having this pleasant spring night. It was doubtful that he'd remember any of them in the morning. Cowboy actually thought that this was his normal state of consciousness, but he was just wiped out on cocaine. When his nostrils were filled with coke, the world made sense. When they weren't, not much made any sense at all.

He was flat on his back, staring at the bright Louisiana night. His body was full of sensation, his mind raced. It could be a really awesome mind when he had coke. Just awesome what thoughts he could have.

It didn't happen too often any more, he mused, what with the fucking puritan shit that Beeker insisted on. Military alert at all times! Hell. He'd left the service years ago, it and all the memories of 'Nam. He didn't need to think about discipline. Besides, this was the modern age, a time when electronics and other forms of technology had made all that macho shit worthless. Except don't tell Beeker that. No, sir.

Cowboy had always loved planes. Always. And the only discipline he'd ever put himself under was the discipline necessary to understand what made things fly. When he graduated from Texas A&M and signed up to fly for the Air Force he had an engineering degree in his hand—a credential that easily got him into the modern service. He knew electronics and he knew what made things stay up in the air when your gut told you they ought to be plummeting right straight down through the clouds.

That meant he was a full generation ahead of most people in his understanding of computer science. As soon as he had understood that computers were going to help things fly, Cowboy had learned all about them. He had never forgotten those first lessons. Computers advanced so fast that another generation was raised up while you were out taking a leak—but Cowboy kept up with it.

That's why, right now, the hundred and ninety-two acres of land outside Shreveport was one of the most sophisticated fortresses in North America. Cowboy had taken his lessons—and the considerable fortune accumulated by the Black Berets in their first missions —and he had devised a state-of-the-art security system. That and more.

Cowboy closed his eyes, and concentrated on his body for a few minutes. If he could concentrate on his thoughts for a full minute and a half, he was sure he would be able to count every one of his muscles. And make up new names for 'em, off the top of his head. God, that was the great thing about having money, he thought. You could buy as much coke as you wanted. The great thing about coke was that it let you *think*.

Damn good thing he had that computer system, he mused. One of its other purposes was to provide Tsali with a means to communicate with the rest of the world when the Berets were in the field. The kid had learned fast. Very fast. Tsali had a natural aptitude for the stuff. Now that he was going away . . . Wow! that was heavy too. Cowboy tightened his closed eyes. Poor kid, in a fucking military school. Boys weren't likely to go easy on a kid who was a full-blooded Indian, and mute to boot. Goddamn if any of those snotty-nosed fuckers—

Tsali could take care of himself.

That thought cheered Cowboy. He grinned and opened his eyes and saw stars. Real stars in the black Louisiana sky. He did more coke.

Cowboy adored Tsali. They all did. But Cowboy had his special relationship. After all, it had been Cowboy who'd arranged for the boy to pop his cherry with that whore down in New Neuzen. Hell, you don't forget the man who arranges something like that for you. It seemed like it had just happened the other day, really. Now Tsali was in New Orleans for the beginning of the summer session at the snob school and they weren't going to see him for weeks at a time. *Shit!*

Well, at least the kid had his keyboard and his modem hook-up so he could contact them whenever he wanted to, Cowboy thought. Poor kid, not being able to speak. But that was one of the wonders of modern technology. Probably in a few years, Cowboy concluded, no one will have to talk at all. We'll all walk around with little keyboards and LED readout screens and that'll be all. He giggled, imagining the expression on some skirt's face when Tsali showed her his readout: *Wanna fuck?*

Oh, didn't *anybody* wanna fuck? Cowboy lifted his pelvis up off the soft floor of the pine forest where he was sprawled and offered himself to some imagined lady who just happened to be wandering through the pine forest. Some *Spanish* lady. *Come to me, señorita. Come and get my hot burrito. It's stuffed with spicy pork. . . .*

He jumped up. Damn cocaine was getting him all hot and bothered and there wasn't a damn woman in miles. *Miles.* What a waste, to get so loaded and not have anyone to play with. Well, damn Beeker, maybe now that they had the extra land and the whole farm was set up so well, maybe now he'd loosen up and let the guys have some fun once in a while.

It wasn't right, Cowboy thought as he made his way back to the farmhouse. It wasn't right for grown men to be denied a grown man's pleasures. Shit, what harm would a little coke do to somebody like Cowboy anyway?

Like the booze and marijuana that Beeker even denied Rosie. Hell, Rosie sneaked that stuff more than Cowboy sneaked his coke. As soon as Beeker was out of sight, Rosie was lighting up. Rosie always volunteered to drive into town because he smoked a joint on the way. Rosie could even smoke dope in a dark corner of some of the black bars he occasionally visited in Shreveport. Cowboy couldn't do that with coke. Why was coke supposed to be more dangerous than dope, Cowboy wondered. Didn't make any sense, no sense at all, he concluded, as he walked face first into a tree.

Cowboy was right. Roosevelt Boone was high as a kite himself. He had scored some great dope in downtown Shreveport. Not the best shit in the world—that was in 'Nam, and if you had to go to 'Nam to get it, Rosie would do without. But this was *fine* shit. Must be Colombian.

That thought pleased Rosie. He smiled as his body relaxed along the length of the big couch in the living room. He sucked on the fat joint he'd lighted for himself. Colombian. Just like Beeker to pull a stunt like that with the New Orleans set-up. Where could Rosie get the best marijuana in the Western Hemisphere? Colombia. Where could Cowboy get the best cocaine? Colombia. So when a bunch of Colombians try to arrange some convenient delivery via ship, what does Beeker do? Their friend and buddy? Their leader? He blows the whole fucking thing right up in the sky. Beeker lets Marty Applebaum loose with some bombs and it's good-bye cocaine, so long mary jane. Wouldn't even let old Cowboy and Rosie go along to take home a few samples.

Okay, Rosie thought, so Delilah says it's the wrong people bringing it in. Bad guys who are going to use their profits in some way that Delilah doesn't think they should. Of course, the Black Berets have yet to have a really good reason to trust that white woman—but then, they haven't had a reason not to. Yet . . . Rosie thought about that for a while. Intense, very intense. Here they are, the five of them and Tsali, and they only trust one other person in the whole world and it's a woman. They don't even know who she works for. She's too smart to say "Trust me." She just goes

23

along on the assumption they do. And they go along with that. Intense, very intense.

Rosie didn't even turn his head when Cowboy stumbled into the house. He listened as the flyer moved around in the kitchen. The cooking area was separated from the enormous living room only by a waist-high counter. A baronial dining table was set up between the couch where Rosie was sprawled and the kitchen where Cowboy was pawing through the refrigerator.

Damn, Tsali had been so funny when they'd built this house, Rosie thought. Turned out the kid had never in his life had anything that was new. He even got excited by the big stainless-steel kitchen appliances that were delivered in crates direct from the manufacturers. Boy had never even *seen* a big-screen color television either, not until Cowboy made Beeker buy one. Sad, turned out the kid had never had his own room either. Then, just like the rest of them, Tsali had a stark barrack-like cubicle—a single cot, a dresser, a chair, and that was that. They all shared a common shower room, more like something you'd find in a gymnasium than in a house, but that was the way Beeker had wanted it. So that was the way it was.

This big living area is sort of nice, Rosie thought—big fireplace, stone floors, and pretty enough that you'd never know the walls were thick enough to withstand anything but a bull's-eye nuclear attack. Then the cubicles and shared spaces. Acres and acres of land outside the house—was Beeker *ever* gonna stop buying it up? All this was possible because every time the Black Berets went into the field on some mission they ended up with even more money in their bank accounts. Except now they had so much that bank accounts weren't good enough. Delilah had become their banker, investing it in God-knew-what sort of shit. But they had a list of numbered accounts in goddamn Switzerland, like they were gangsters or dictators or something. And who was he? he asked himself. Just plain old Rosie Boone, who used to skin corpses.

The telephone rang, and Rosie was somewhere near it, so he answered it.

It was a woman. *Is Mr. Beeker there?*

"Nope," said Rosie politely, and hung up.

The telephone rang again while Rosie was rolling another bomber joint. "Hey Cowboy, your turn," said Rosie. "Some lady. So it's for you."

Cowboy wandered over and picked up the telephone.

Is Mr. Beeker there and please don't hang up.

"Nope," said Cowboy, but he didn't hang up.

Ah, this is a business matter.

"We don't need no more business," said Cowboy. "Had enough business for a while. Want to rest. All of us."

Who am I talking to?

"Sherwood Thatcher Cowboy. No wait, Hatcher. Cowboy Sherwood Thatcher Hatcher. Call me Cowboy."

Mr. Cowboy, I'm calling about Mr. Beeker's letter to Mexotex—

"Oh yeah, we love Mexitex's burritos," said Cowboy. "Filled with spicy pork."

Mexotex isn't a fast food chain, Mr. Cowboy. It's a gas company. We're about to lay pipeline across property recently purchased by Mr. Beeker, and this past week we received a letter asking that the option be foregone, and offering us—

"I got a great burrito," said Cowboy. He grinned at Rosie, and pointed lewdly at his crotch.

Mr. Cowboy—

"Never had no complaints on my spicy pork burrito," said Cowboy. "You want my recipe?"

What I want is to talk to Mr. Beeker. Is there somewhere I can reach him?

"He's in New Orleans. But you can talk to me. Me and Beak are like this." Cowboy held up two fingers tightly together.

Like what?

"Like *this*," Cowboy repeated. "Oh right, this is a telephone. You can't see me. Good, 'cause my pants just fell off. But you can talk to me. I do Beak's business. I sign his papers. I write his letters. I wrote that letter so I know what you're talking about."

"You liar," said Rosie peaceably from the couch. "You lie like a Texan, Cowboy. I never heard this kind of shit. Man you are fucked-up." He handed the joint to Cowboy, who sucked on it hard.

We're not getting anywhere. It's really crucial that I—

"You like champagne?"

Champagne?

"You want to come out here tomorrow and have a champagne brunch? I heard that on *Magnum P.I.* Magnum invited this woman for a champagne brunch and then he laid her."

A champagne brunch on Tuesday morning? In Shreveport?

"Dom—Dom something."

Dom Pérignon.

"Hey, right. Ten o'clock. Hey, this Dom shit has got the tiniest bubbles you ever saw. You ain't never seen nothing like it. And we'll talk about pipelines and burritos and all that shit."

Tomorrow morning, Mr. Cowboy? Are you sure you'll remember?

"Oh sure—what's your name?"

Isabella Cifuentes.

"Oh yeah," said Cowboy, grinning at Rosie. "Oh *yeah,* Señorita Cifuentes—you and me—that's what we're gonna do in the morning. We're gonna talk about laying some pipe. You and me."

Ten o'clock, Mr. Cowboy. A champagne brunch.

She hung up the telephone.

Cowboy rubbed his hands together. "Oh yeah, Rosie, must have been a whole goddamn month since I laid me some pipe. . . ."

4

Roosevelt Boone woke up with the bright sun shining through the windows of the Louisiana farmhouse. He had a smile on his face. His sleep had been deep, far from the battles that he and the other Black Berets had fought. His dreams had been a succession of encounters with beautiful black women, the kind with juicy smiles, high-stepping butts, and willing dispositions. Outside, a family of finches chirped and foraged and battled in the shrubbery. Rosie could smell the rich Louisiana earth. This was the way life was supposed to be.

Rosie stretched out. His heavily muscled arms quickly tightened to produce an outsized image of maleness. He collapsed back onto the couch and only then saw the destruction.

Cowboy was sprawled out on the floor at the foot of the couch. Around him were four empty bottles of champagne. Corks and labels were scattered as well. "Jesus Christ," Rosie snorted. One of Cowboy's problems with cocaine was that it laid him open to other indulgences. He lost his sense of measurement about alcohol and pussy.

Rosie stood up and grabbed Cowboy under his armpits. The flyer didn't respond as Rosie dragged him down the corridor toward the communal lavatory. Cowboy's heels bumped over each of the small steps that led down into the shower area.

"Thank God Beeker ain't here to see this," Rosie said aloud as he turned on the cold shower full blast.

Even the icy flow of water didn't have an immediate effect on the flyer. His stuporous body retained its immobility for a few beats. But when the cold water did finally intrude into Cowboy's consciousness, it did so with a vengeance.

"What the fuck . . ."

Cowboy sat up straight and then froze. His hands slowly moved up to his head, as though to protect it from something much more painful than mere cold water. "Ohhhhhh . . ." He stayed in place for at least a minute before he crawled out of the frigid spray.

"Coffee." The word was plaintively spoken. It was not a request but a plea. "Coffee." As yet, he didn't even seem to know that Rosie was there.

The litany of the single word was still going on when Rosie returned in a couple of minutes. He had zapped some water in the microwave to help quicken the production of some instant brew. A pot of the real stuff was being made, but until it was ready this would have to do.

Rosie held it in front of Cowboy's face. The steam rose toward Cowboy's nostrils. Once there the aroma was enough to allow the blond man's eyes to open.

"Jesus," whispered Rosie. He was honestly shocked. Cowboy's eyeballs were more red than white. The tiny veins seemed to bulge. If Cowboy cried right now, Rosie swore he'd be weeping blood instead of tears.

"Glasses." Cowboy got that word out after a sip of the coffee. Rosie knew at once what his buddy needed. Cowboy was only rarely seen without his dark glasses. Even in dimly lit bars the man kept his shades on. It must have been torture for him not to have them protecting his eyes at this minute.

The big black man raced to the front room and found where Cowboy had tossed them. He brought them back to the shower. Cowboy had finished the instant coffee. Now Rosie put on the glasses and then carefully pried the mug out of Cowboy's rictored fingers. He stood Cowboy up and quickly stripped the man of his clothing. Now naked—except for the dark glasses—Cowboy was pushed back under the shower head and once again the water was turned on. This time it was warm. Even over the rush of the

28

shower Rosie heard the litany, a little expanded now. "Coffee, Rosie. More coffee . . ."

. . . *beep* . . . *beep* . . . *beep* . . .

"Oh God, stop that noise," Cowboy begged. "Please Rosie, that noise . . ."

. . . *beep* . . . *beep* . . . *beep* . . .

Rosie stood and moved toward the control room where the Black Berets housed their security system. He looked down at one of the green screens and watched a dot moving along the driveway with careful regularity. A car. He flipped a switch and the sound went off.

"A fucking deer," Cowboy said as he sipped still another cup of coffee. It was the beginning of the second pot this morning. He realized he couldn't really complain about the noise—after all, he had been the one who had installed the system. It had been his own insistence that created the beast. They had all agreed that something of the sort was necessary. They were in the field too often with Tsali left alone. The kid needed the security for protection; the Black Berets were getting to be too well known. There were people gunning for them. They had to have the security. But the system was so sophisticated, with high-tech sensors all over the perimeter of the land Beeker owned, that it would pick up the movement of anything as large as a six-year-old child.

Cowboy figured that anyone smaller than that was unlikely to be a trained assassin.

"No deer," Rosie said when he returned, "it's your brunch date."

"Date?" Cowboy was incredulous. He was sitting at the dining room table wearing nothing but his briefs and his sunglasses. "At ten o'clock in the morning?"

"Yep. The woman who called last night. From that pipeline company. The one you talked dirty to."

"Shit," Cowboy breathed.

"Better go get pretty for her," Rosie advised. "She'll be here in about three minutes."

Cowboy staggered off toward his room. A few minutes later he returned, wearing his jeans and one of the many pairs of hand-tooled boots that he had accumulated in his prosperity. He had on a yoked cowboy shirt, though it was the least colorful of all the ones he owned. He would have had on a second pair of sunglasses if he could have figured out how to fit them over the first pair. When he walked out into the big living area of the house he had to stop. Even with the shades the bright light was momentarily blinding.

The visitor had arrived, but Cowboy couldn't see her. She was already seated in a high-backed chair, turned away from him. All he could see of her was an outstretched hand holding a champagne glass. Rosie was pouring.

"Here you go. Cowboy says champagne brunch, you gonna get champagne brunch."

Cowboy gagged, certain that if he didn't concentrate he'd start to dry-heave. He wished Rosie would put that bottle away.

Cowboy staggered over to a chair that faced the visitor. Cowboy wondered if she'd told him her name on the telephone last night. Cowboy couldn't remember last night, much less what he'd heard or said on the phone. He eased himself down on the chair slowly to alleviate the shock of the contact of his body with the furniture. Only when he was safely in place did he look up.

Then it was as though some long-forgotten god had descended and placed a healing hand on Cowboy's skull. The pain was gone. Just like that.

"This is Cowboy," said Rosie to their guest. "Don't talk too loud."

"Isabella Cifuentes," the woman said, and held out her hand. She was small, almost tiny, and had to sit on the edge of her chair to come even close to meeting Cowboy half-way. Cowboy loved her tiny hands and their sharp nails, painted bright red. He loved her black hair, and her full red lips. He loved what she did to that dress she was wearing. "I'm president of Mexotex Oil and Gas," she said.

Cowboy couldn't protect his hangover from the pounding his body took in the Jeep as it jostled its way over the terrain that was

30

Beeker's new land. The Jeep bounced and jumped along the path that Cowboy could barely make out. The track could hardly be called a road. Cowboy imagined that at one point it had been used by one of the logging companies that harvest Louisiana timber. There hadn't been any need for a smooth highway then, and now there was even less. Anything that hadn't had four-wheel drive would never have made this journey. The Jeep was having a hard enough time of it as it was.

Cowboy wasn't willing to admit the painful extent of his returning hangover to Isabella Cifuentes. He kept his face in an unmoving, slightly smiling mask. A man like Cowboy may have great self-indulgences—the cocaine, the Spanish women he loved to love, the passion for flying—but Cowboy and the likes of him were also those men who, through some trait so deeply embedded that it might have been genetic, also had the ability to come alert if it was necessary. If the alarm had sounded in earnest that morning—before Cowboy's shower and the two pots of coffee—Cowboy would have jumped up among the empty champagne bottles, grabbed his M16, and been ready for whatever was coming at them. But that was a life-or-death situation. Isabella Cifuentes was gorgeous—the only thing better than a Spanish lady was a *small* Spanish lady so far as Cowboy was concerned—but she wasn't life-or-death. The woman talked, and Cowboy listened. His crotch ached from the constraints of the layers of cloth, and the hangover pounded in his head.

Mexotex wanted to pipe natural gas out of the impoverished northeastern quadrant of Mexico, through Texas and Louisiana, and up into the energy-starved northeastern corner of the United States. Not only would this new pipeline provide necessary fuel to New York and New England, it would increase competition among already operating gas companies. And it just might keep a few hundred thousand Mexican citizens from starving to death in the next decade.

Cowboy had seen the poverty of much of Latin America, a poverty so grinding that it was beyond the comprehension of most Americans who thought being poor was watching a black-and-white television or having to eat beans and franks a couple of nights a week. That wasn't poverty by Latin American standards —that was unreachable wealth.

The Mexotex plan sounded good to Cowboy. Ms. Cifuentes was one of those liberal entrepreneurs who was trying to use her company to make a profit. She wasn't going to deny that, but she also believed that the company could do some social good while it was at it. Cowboy had taken in the data without making too many judgments of his own—but now he'd decided that it made sense in most ways.

Most ways but one. There was no way in hell that that pipeline was going to cross Billy Leaps Beeker's property. Unless . . .

The Jeep came to a halt. Cowboy took a look at the map. "This is it."

They climbed out of the vehicle and looked around for a few moments. They were in the midst of a scrub pine forest. It had been harvested for the last time about fifteen years before, and not replanted. The growth since then had been vigorous and plentiful, but the vegetation was for the most part useless, diseased pine and dense, prickly underbrush. Over to the right was an area that had been ignited by lightning a season or two back.

"Your pipeline would go right down the middle of this." Cowboy gestured broadly with his right arm.

"I know," said the president of Mexotex. "I scouted this area months ago. I'm not just a boardroom president, Mr. Cowboy."

"No ma'am," said Cowboy grinning. "But I ought to tell you, I don't think Mr. Beeker's gonna be too happy about you coming in here with your pipeline."

"I understand that perfectly," said Isabella easily. "I imagine it will be a frustrating experience for him. But the fact is, we have the option, and we're going to exercise it."

"He'll pay, I don't think there's—"

"That doesn't matter," Isabella said. "Because we simply have no alternative. Everything in that direction"—she pointed toward the north—"either belongs to Ranger Petroleum directly, or they've bought the option on it. They did that, Mr. Cowboy, in order to keep us from laying our pipe. We're suing them for restraint of trade, of course, but in the meantime, I intend for our pipeline to go through. And I intend for it to go through *here*. Our machines are about three miles to the west of here. Mr. Beeker, I suppose, could make a certain amount of difficulty for us—"

"Mr. Beeker can make a whole lot of difficulty when he sets his mind to it," said Cowboy. "His mind's pretty set on this issue, is one thing I know. Of course I could talk to him a little—"

"I wish you would."

"—*if* I was to get the right kind of encouragement from you, señorita."

She looked Cowboy directly in the eye. "We have a very strict rule against bribery, Mr. Cowboy."

"Just plain old Cowboy, ma'am, and I'm not talking about money. Money I don't need, and neither does Beeker. No, I was talking—"

He snaked his arm about her waist. Her ass was as firm as he could have hoped. The inside of his elbow brushed against her breasts. They were tightly encased in a stiff brassiere. He liked that trussed-in feeling on a woman. The tighter in they were, the more exciting they were when they got unhooked. She smiled up at him, a slight smile, not precisely encouraging, it was true, but a smile nonetheless.

He lowered his lips to hers. This one was going to be easy, he thought—

—until she bit him.

Bit him *hard*. He tried to draw back but couldn't. She'd caught his lower lip in her teeth and she wasn't letting go. He felt blood fill his mouth. He knew the taste. He put his hands on her upper arms with the intention of squeezing her till she released him, but by that time she'd already unlocked her teeth and drawn back.

She kept the smile. "I'm not a whore. I won't buy you off, Mr. Cowboy. And I won't barter my body for a good word from you to Mr. Beeker. Mr. Beeker will allow the pipeline to go through this very remote corner of his property for two reasons. The first reason is that, by law, he has to. The second reason is that it would be a good thing for him to do—for the people of this country, and for the people of Mexico."

Cowboy held the back of his hand tightly against his mouth. He

33

still winced with the pain of his new wound. It hurt almost enough to take his mind off his hangover.

"I'll drive back to the house, Mr. Cowboy, and we'll find something for your little accident."

He screamed when she poured a cupful of hydrogen peroxide into his mouth. Isabella and Rosie stood on either side of his chair, staring down at him as if he were an ill-behaved boy who'd just gotten beat up on the playground. "Here's my card," she said to Rosie. "Give me a call, will you please, when Mr. Beeker returns. I'd like to speak to him directly." She walked out of the house without another word.

"So," said Rosie, sticking the card in the pocket of Cowboy's shirt, "when's the ceremony?"

5

The only one of the group who might have had a right to act the part of a petulant child was doing anything but.

Tsali stood mute as always, but just as respectful as always, too, in the office of the Reverend Marchand Delaroche. Beeker and Delilah were seated in the comfortable chairs that faced the dean's desk. Delaroche was behind it, puffing on a pipe in a manner so theatrical that none of the three believed he had any enjoyment from it. He was fortunately at the end of a long drone about the traditions of the Academy of the Holy Sword.

"While we are, of course, one of the oldest and most respected institutions for young men in the Old South, we have left behind the unfortunate practices and prejudices of previous eras." Delaroche looked at Tsali, not for the first time. "There is certainly no longer any hint of racial discrimination in our entrance policies. However, it might have been . . . *propitious* if you had let us know about the young man's . . . ethnic background."

Delilah counted to five slowly. If Beeker shot off before that there would be no help for the minister. She looked at Delaroche and shook her head slowly. *What a stupid thing to say to a man like Beeker. You might just get killed for saying something as stupid as that.*

Beeker's knuckles were white from the pressure of the grip he was putting on the arms of his chair. His jaw was locked tight. His concern for Tsali's reaction was the only thing that kept him from jumping over the desk and strangling Delaroche.

He looked at the boy who was standing between him and Delilah. Tsali's face bore no expression. The kid's eyes moved to meet Beeker's and there was a twinkle in them. Beeker knew what that meant immediately. *Asshole*. Beeker relaxed back into the chair. If that was the way Tsali wanted to play it, fine by him. The kid was right. People like Delaroche were just plain assholes and it wasn't worth throttling them every time they displayed the characteristics of the species.

Still, it bothered Beeker. What if this kind of thinking were reflected in the policies and day-to-day activities of the school? What if Tsali had to deal with ignorant white prejudice every time he turned around? Hell, the boy had been on the farm only a few months. Sure, he had all the training he needed to take care of himself in battle against any other boy—or almost any unarmed, professional soldier the United States military could produce right now, for that matter.

But what about the hurt of words? The hurt of contempt? The kind of shit that couldn't be fought against by fists alone? Beeker sighed. Hell, Tsali had been getting that all his life. It wouldn't be anything new to him. Maybe the words would be a little more subtle, more refined, but after a kid's spent most of his life in foster homes and juvenile centers, there wasn't much new in cruelty under the sun.

"Now, there will be no problem, I assure you of that," said the Reverend Marchand Delaroche. "I'll simply make sure that his room assignment—"

"Reverend Delaroche," began Delilah, interrupting with a smile. She had just lighted a cigarette and the curl of smoke was thick about her face. "This does seem to be a strange attitude for an institution supported and maintained by a church."

Delaroche clamped on his pipe. The scent of tobacco was strong and sickly sweet. "Damn liberals took over the church long ago. Long, long ago. What we're doing here is going back to the basic principles that made the church and the nation great. And these principles are discipline, discipline, and discipline."

Delilah waited a moment before replying, "Let me make this very plain to you. The Academy of the Holy Sword was chosen for three reasons. First, because Mr. Beeker and I are anxious for Tsali to have a good education in the context of a military academy. The second reason is the Academy's proximity to Mr. Beeker's estate in Shreveport. It was also important that the Academy be a place where a man of Mr. Beeker's wealth could be sure of his son's personal security."

As Delilah inhaled on her cigarette, she noted that the statement was having its effect on Delaroche. They were all alike, she decided, these men who claimed to stand for the best in education, in business, in politics—even in religion. In fact, they were venal creatures, impressed with money, swayed by any perception of importance.

Delilah knew that Delaroche had probably been bewildered by the manner in which the connection with Beeker and his adopted son had been made. No matter how shocked the dean had been by the presence of a full-blooded, mute Cherokee boy in his office, that impression must have been tempered by remembering that the introduction had come from some of the very highest circles in Washington. A member of the Joint Chiefs of Staff had telephoned Delaroche personally. Delilah was reminding him, making sure he didn't think the situation was one that had anything to do with the Bureau of Indian Affairs. She'd aimed at getting him back to the voice he had heard on the phone—one so high up he had only dreamed of ever hearing it personally—to make sure he understood that Beeker was a very rich man. Tsali would have no problems after that, she thought.

Though Delilah's little game soured Beeker, he let her play it. Tsali watched just as carefully, and with far greater enjoyment.

Delaroche puffed dramatically on his pipe and finally began to speak again. "One of the reasons the Academy of the Holy Sword exists is to ensure that certain members of the country's . . . *elite* receive the discipline that only early military training can provide."

"Tsali won't need a military academy to give him discipline. He's got that now." Beeker was adamant. He had crossed his arms over his chest, a gesture he seldom used but which served as an emphatic reminder of his Cherokee heritage. Delilah stared at the man and swore she could see him in a loincloth on the plains more easily than in the over-decorated, stuffy office of a private school dean. "Tsali's going to a military school 'cause he's already used to military life," Beeker concluded. "Anything else'd turn him soft."

Delaroche replied with undisguised condescension. "Well, Mr. Beeker, I think it would be better if we had our cards all out on the table. Most parents in this day and age don't send their children to Holy Sword because their offspring are used to military discipline —they send them because they've never had anything like a strong guiding hand. I've read your son's records, and I must confess that his . . . *tendencies* are quite apparent."

"Tendencies?" Beeker echoed slowly.

"Toward . . ." Delaroche paused for just the right phrase. "Moral dereliction" is what he came up with. "That is why we have asked you to sign the waiver allowing us to administer corporal punishment, whenever we deem corporal punishment for the boy's welfare and proper development."

Beeker glanced up at his son. Tsali only smiled. Whatever the Academy of the Holy Sword came up with in the way of rules and regulations weren't going to faze the boy.

Riding away from the Academy of the Holy Sword in the back of Delilah's hired limousine, Delilah looked at Beeker. She saw his discomfort and moved over across the wide seat and wrapped an arm around one of his. "Don't worry. Tsali won't be dealing with Delaroche. The instruction really is supposed to be very good. Tsali will be fine."

"That asshole got to me. I don't think I should have left Tsali there." Beeker wouldn't look at her nor would he soften the expression on his face. "Kid doesn't need that kind of shit. Social snobs, silly military games, fat and stupid dean—"

"Beeker, stop it. Look, you wouldn't have been happy with Tsali going anywhere, anywhere at all. Nothing would have satisfied you. But he needs to go to school and he needs to get to know other boys his own age. Now, we pulled every string in Washington to arrange this. The school's a good one, it's close to Shreveport, and it's the right place for Tsali. The summer term is short, and after a month he'll be allowed home on the weekends. And the thing you've got to remember is that Tsali can take care of himself. That's what you've tried to teach him."

"What if he can't?" Beeker hated even to entertain the idea—it was what he feared most about this whole business.

"Then he'll just have to learn how," said Delilah.

Beeker knew she was right.

Tsali would never have shown his real feelings to Beeker. There was one set of emotions that gnawed deep within him, but he kept it to himself.

As he stood in his room, his new home in the academy, he looked at the four identical beds and the matching chests of drawers and the rest of the furniture—more opulent than anything he'd had at home in Shreveport, though the Academy considered the room Spartan. Tsali fought against his emotion.

After sixteen years of being shunted from halfway house to foster home, from juvenile center to time on the streets, Tsali had found a home with Beeker and the rest of the Black Berets. There was a primal fear that this was another step on the road to nowhere he had always been traveling. It meant that the farm and the men there hadn't been a real home—his goal after so many years of just moving on—but just another rest area, much more pleasant than the others but no more enduring.

There was no reason, he told himself, to think that. He knew that Billy Leaps Beeker was now his legal father. He knew that Cowboy thought he was a little brother and that the others cared for him as well. But he couldn't get over a dismal sense of abandonment. He had hoped that was a feeling entirely in his past, an emotion he'd never have to deal with again.

It was here, in this room with him.

He didn't want to go to a fucking boarding school, he thought. He wanted to go back to Shreveport and hunt with his father. Sneak out for a beer with Cowboy. Kids his own age? How could he relate to kids his own age after the past months, months when he had been a real warrior, not a scrubbed, dress-up soldier.

He'd share this room with three other boys.

39

What would they say when they discovered he was a full-blooded Cherokee?

What would they think when they found out he was mute?

What would they do if they knew that Tsali had been responsible for the deaths of half a dozen grown men?

How would they deal with him, and how would he deal with them?

He sat down at the small wooden desk and took out a sheet of stationery in the top drawer. It had the legend *Academy of the Holy Sword* in large script letters over an embossed seal of the school.

With a pen held steady by force of will, Tsali wrote:

Dear Father:
I like this place very much already. I am sorry it is costing you so much money, but I will try to make you proud of me . . .

6

The Louisiana Superdome rises up on the banks of the Mississippi River. It makes all of New Orleans's claims to being a historic, gracious city a lie. The truth of the matter is apparent in this huge, domed stadium. New Orleans may keep a few neighborhoods in careful preservation for the tourists, but for itself, it wanted a football team—a National Football League team. For that it was willing to construct a monstrosity of concrete and plastic, acres of parking lots, and a field of Astroturf.

New Orleans is as American as apple pie, but apple pie isn't a French Quarter. Apple pie is a major league franchise underwritten by taxpayers' dollars. All the history in the world wouldn't have satisfied New Orleans's civic pride, but the New Orleans Saints did.

The local governments that oversaw the establishment and construction of the Superdome were desperate to make the monstrosity pay off. They'd have hired the thing out to anyone who could afford it, stopping only perhaps at a meeting of the International Communist Conspiracy. But this time they'd struck real paydirt. They'd found a lessee for a week who was as apple pie American as anyone would ever want. PAL—Prepared Americans League.

"Harry! It's fucking fabulous! It's fucking heaven!"

It took a Marty Applebaum to appreciate the collection of arms and attitude that PAL had brought together under this one soaring roof. There were exhibits from nearly every arms manufacturer in

41

the world—at least the free world. Helicopters, small arms, automatic rifles—all of it was there.

Harry had thought that a trip to Las Vegas would be good enough to reward Marty for his job on that dope ship. But Cowboy and Rosie had discovered this private circus much closer to home. They were right, of course—this was just what Marty wanted, everything he could hope for in a vacation. A million and one ways to blow the world to kingdom come.

Marty had insisted that they dress for the occasion. Harry had hesitated, but the little blond man's enthusiasm had been right on target. Every man in the place was decked out in quasi-military gear, trying to give the impression that he belonged to some kind of mercenary organization. Compared to them Harry's and Marty's Black Berets' uniforms were understated and drab.

"Beeker wouldn't like us wearing this stuff," Harry said. Actually *he* didn't like wearing it. It was a sacred act for Harry to put on the dark fatigues that Beeker had had sewn for the men. Sacred because it seemed that every other time they'd put on these clothes they had ended up killing people—a lot of people. If you put on your killing clothes and you don't kill, he thought, you get frustrated.

"Hell, I don't care!" Marty insisted. "No one fucking knows what a great job we do. No one! It's a fucking shame. Here we can at least be with guys who *care!* Harry, if these guys knew the shit we've pulled, we'd be fucking heroes to them, the way we should be. Hell, after that ship in the harbor yesterday—"

"*Shhhhhh!*" Harry gestured madly. "You can't talk about that stuff!"

"Yeah, well . . ." Marty kicked at a wall. "People should know about it. These people here, they'd care about it. What the fuck, let's look around. Let's see what they've got to offer. Maybe we can get some ideas for the Berets."

Marty was right. The people at the PAL convention would have cared. They were, for the most part, men who had experienced the adventure of battle and now felt incomplete without the sense of camaraderie, danger, fulfillment, and personal consequence that war had provided them. Young and old, they'd traveled from all over the South—and from much farther afield—to look over this awesome collection of goods, to attend the many workshops that had been set up, to reunite with old friends, and to make new ones. In many cases the men brought their girlfriends, and even their wives and children. The PAL convention contrived to take care of them all. To the rest of the world it might have seemed a peculiar sort of family outing, but goddammit, he thought, the thing *worked*.

As the two Black Berets walked up and down the aisles of the convention, it quickly became apparent to the Greek that Marty could talk all he wanted to. That was obviously the main thing that this place offered—talk. Because if a tiny fraction of what Harry overheard was true, then the world would have been destroyed ten times over and half of the population of Vietnam would have been dragged out of Asia by covert operations the men in this place had undertaken in just the past six months.

Harry hadn't heard so much bullshit in years. It was crazy. It was like being caught in the middle of a thousand Applebaums, each one desperate to outdo his neighbor with a story whose slender bone of reality was so obscured by the bloated telling that it could never again be found.

"I left my two best buddies in Afghanistan. . . ."

"Sure, the Cubans caught me in Angola—but I got out, didn't I? Escaped three times . . ."

"I tell you—one more trip into Nicaragua and the whole place will fall apart. . . ."

"Three of us, we got this plan, so when you hear that they're picking up little pieces of Khaddafi all over North Africa . . ."

These were some of the outrageous stories Harry heard as they roamed through the place. It was funny to watch how Marty reacted. Because Marty's stories were just as outrageous—but absolutely true—Marty assumed that everybody else was telling the truth as well.

There was nobody so naive as a true killer.

The Greek stood patiently by as Marty stopped at each and every booth to look over whatever new or repackaged item an arms manufacturer had for sale. Marty's favorite was a laser sight available for mounting on M16's. "Great idea!" Marty had congratulated the salesman. "Hey Harry, we need these guys *bad*. Beeker will flip. You can just point the thing in the middle of the night—"

"And if you miss the first shot, the bastard you're shooting at will have a hundred-yard beam that is pointing right at your eyeball," Harry scoffed. It was one of the few times that the Greek interfered with Marty's fun. He was tolerant of Applebaum's adventures for the most part, but he wasn't about to let Marty foist inferior or useless hardware on the team.

No one had ever figured out quite why Harry was so good about tolerating Marty's antics, but he was. There was a deep well of good nature behind the Greek's stony facade. People seldom realized that, because they were never able to look beyond the intense sadness commingled with anger that brimmed in Harry's eyes like tears in the eyes of a war widow. The expression gave witness to such a mortal loss experienced some time in the past that the usual response was to allow Harry a wide berth. Maybe, just maybe, Harry's tolerance of Marty came from the same place.

The two of them had, after all, gone through a lot together. They'd both been in the Navy SEALs. They'd done special training together and they'd been with one another when Beeker found them drinking in an off-limits dump in Da Nang. The Cherokee had made them part of the most awesome fighting group of the war.

Things had happened to people in Vietnam. Things that changed who they were. Sometimes men couldn't hide those changes. Harry almost never could. Marty, though, never internalized his feelings the way the Greek did. Applebaum always let everything loose. Most people would have called that obnoxious. It was. But that was the way Marty was, so it was okay with Harry.

So Harry followed Applebaum through the orderly aisles of displays and watched languidly as the crowds of uniformed men, and a few women, passed by. Many of them clung to a daydream about what Vietnam had been. They still dressed in the uniforms of that era, but the only battle they were fighting now was against middle-aged spread. And they were losing.

It all made Harry sad. Because while Marty was looking at weapons, Harry was looking at the other things that were for sale.

Patches and insignia for units that never existed.

Freeze-dried food that cost half as much if it was bought in Montgomery Ward or Sears.

Cammies that were blends—and would trap your perspiration rather than letting it bleed through, the way more expensive cotton did.

Rope that was twice as expensive and half as good as what you could get in a corner hardware store.

Maps on microfiche that would be impossible to read under even optimal circumstances—much less under any sort of duress.

A thousand items that were uselessly painted, or printed, or dyed in green, gray, olive, and black. He even saw a pregnant woman in a camouflage maternity outfit, and he read a notice on a bulletin board inviting everyone to attend a camouflage wedding that night.

The manufacturers were bleeding these good people dry, Harry thought, and it made him sad.

He thought about all the old veterans who once a year brought out their stuff for the Memorial Day parade and strutted down Main Street in one last attempt to rekindle lost glory, lost heroism, lost youth. Vietnam was now slipping into the past. There was a whole generation growing up that didn't know where it was, much less what it was about. These men couldn't give up their memories.

It made Harry sad, because Harry knew what that was like. He had never given up those memories either.

And never would.

"Marty," he said, before Applebaum could ask him to go a second round among the exhibits, "I need a beer. I need about six."

7

"Hey, great!" said Marty, a little to Harry's surprise. "Maybe we'll run into somebody we know. I bet there are lots of guys from the SEALs here, don't you think so, Harry? Don't you?"

Harry would have liked to return to the hotel, but an arms dealer had given Marty an entrance ticket to one of the private bars located around the top of the Astrodome. Marty, who always liked to appear in the heart of anything, demanded that he and Harry go there instead.

The bar was posh, and there seemed to Harry to be a real difference in the clientele up here from the rest of the convention. These men seemed a little more serious. Some of them were wearing suits, even. And no women. The conversations were quiet, as if the people at the small tables *didn't* want their plans overheard. At first Marty was disappointed by the quietness, but when Harry said to him, "This is where the real action of this convention is going on," Marty decided they'd stay.

After a few moments, Marty said, "Hey, you were right. I see two recruiters in here. Two honest-to-God recruiters."

Harry had already spotted them. He sipped a big frozen mug of beer.

Marty was working the crowd with his eyes. His head turned so rapidly it looked like it was going to swivel clear around if he wasn't careful.

"Jack! Jack Dolan! Over here!" Marty was standing half up off his chair and screaming at some man across the room. Harry sighed again when he heard the name. *Asshole.* Sometimes the world seemed to be populated by nothing else.

The man named Jack Dolan sauntered over to where the two Black Berets were sitting. Harry watched, and saw the moment their identities registered in his brain. His handshake with Marty was tentative, almost grudging. He only exchanged barely perceptible nods with Harry. Marty didn't notice. He went on like a madman.

Sometimes Harry wondered at the extent of Marty's masochism. No other word for it, he thought: Here was one of the prime idiot officers who had tortured Marty every way but hooking him up to a generator, and Marty was still looking up to him. Harry figured it was just that Dolan was the perfect image for the role of hero. He had the looks, nearly as strong and masculine as Beeker's, and he had the scar on his face. He also had the quietly swaggering attitude to match.

"Come on, come on, have a seat and a drink on us." Marty was insistent.

"I'm with a friend," said Dolan. It wasn't a refusal, it was an invitation for the friend to be invited over as well.

"Bring him on over," said Marty expansively. "Let's get something going in here. Dead hole, this place," he said, looking around with ostentatious condescension.

Dolan waved to a man who had lingered at the doorway. The man, who had evidently been waiting for the signal, made his way through the crowd over to the Berets' table. Harry watched him come and just knew that he was just as bad as Dolan was.

"Name is Mason," said Dolan. "J. K. Mason."

Mason was nearly as big as Harry himself. Over six-two and at least the same two hundred pounds. Difference was, this guy was so blond he was nearly albino. The weight was a mass of unformed fat, built on a frame that was good probably twenty years ago—hardly a match for the constantly trained muscle on Harry. When he arrived Dolan introduced them all. Harry didn't stand up, but he did shake the man's hand from his seat.

Dolan and Mason sat down at the table and Marty had a field day officiously waving over a waiter. The men each placed an order. A rum and Coke for Dolan, bourbon and water for Mason. It was a fine opening for Marty. "Now listen," he said loudly to the waiter, "none of your rotgut for my friends. None of your bar-pour shit. I want good stuff, top shelf for everyone and make everybody's a double . . . no, make everybody's a triple, and pour more for Harry and me too. Harry's drinking that expensive German beer, none of the cow's piss you brought over a while ago. And I want the finest Scotch you got. Chivas. Yeah, Chivas and you might as well just bring the whole bottle. I'm gonna need it all now that I found my pals."

Harry's eyes turned behind his lids. First of all, he was just drinking Bud—it's all he drank, it's all he wanted. Second of all, this meant that Marty wasn't going to be satisfied with a little rest stop on their way back to the hotel. That nice big room-service steak was getting farther and farther away. He might as well prepare himself for the duration, he decided.

Wise decision. Carefully sipping his beer through the two hours that followed, he watched with the usual awe as Marty made his way through half a bottle of Scotch. Marty could drink unfathomable amounts of liquor without getting drunk, in fact, without showing any effects of the alcohol. Marty spent his entire mental existence intoxicated with excitement and enthusiasm—liquor and drugs seemed to have no additional effect on him. Mason and Dolan drank almost as deeply as Marty, but made not even one offer to pay for an additional round.

Marty's generosity finally got to Dolan. He grudgingly commented, "Applebaum, looks like you're making out okay." His hand indicated the latest trayful of glasses that the waiter brought over.

"Hey Dolan, I'm doing more than okay." Marty sat back in a weak imitation of a television actor he had once seen in a movie, but his attempt at an expansive gesture was lost because of his tiny size and thin frame. "So's Harry. Harry and me are doing great. Aren't we doing great, Harry?"

"We're living up in Shreveport, on this farm Beeker's got," Harry said.

"Beeker?" echoed Dolan in a tone of annoyance. "That crazy half-breed that got half his ear shot off saving some nigger's life?"

Harry looked around quickly and saw the scowl that developed on Mason's pallored face.

"Yeah, Beak, you remember the Beak," Marty chattered on. "Hell of a guy. Got us all back together again. Me, Harry, Cowboy, Rosie—"

"That was the nigger he saved," said Dolan, drinking from his glass and glancing at his silent companion.

Harry stifled an urge to teach Dolan some manners. Hell, that asshole wasn't worth the scratch Harry might get on his fist.

Mason spoke next, asking Marty, "When you say 'together,' what do you mean?"

"We're a fighting team again, just like we were in 'Nam."

Harry shot his friend a warning glance, but if Marty saw it, he didn't pay any attention.

Mason evidently hadn't paid close attention to his friend's comments against Beeker and Rosie—or else he didn't have quite the same prejudices, or else was just very intrigued with the thought of a resurrected Vietnam force. "Well," he said to Marty, "the only way the world's gonna get saved for decent men is if decent men learn how to fight."

"So long as they *can* fight!" exclaimed Dolan. "We gotta face the facts. The world's gonna go up in a cloud of smoke and the only way to handle it is to be prepared to survive. Survival's what's gonna save the human race."

"How do you figure that?" Harry asked. These guys weren't making any more sense than most assholes, he thought, and probably less. It was too bad. Most of Harry's fund of tolerance that day had already been expended on Marty.

"Look, when the War comes, the guys who prepared for it will win." Mason leaned over the table with a conspiratorial leer. This was evidently his subject, even more than it was Dolan's. "The War is gonna eliminate the impure and the unworthy." He said it as if he were quoting scripture.

How, Harry wondered, could this tub of lard consider himself one of the pure and worthy?

"Those who are strong and intelligent," Mason went on, "those who have the genetic make-up that has made America great—those'll be the ones who survive the War."

"That's right," said Dolan in a soft voice. "Sure as hell."

"We're gonna reform society," said Mason, with the evident assumption that he would be one of the fortunate survivors. "But this time it'll be along the right lines."

"We could do that right now," said Dolan. "If we could just let our men loose. They'd take care of the threat of communism. If we could just let 'em loose. See, the Russians are just commie politicians. They don't want the bomb. The only reason they want to win over here is to get their hands on DisneyWorld and shit like that. They don't want to blow it up. But our politicians don't see it like that. They're already in the commies' hands. They're keeping our men from using their natural superiority on the enemy. That's why it's so important we have PAL. So we can field our own troops —when the time comes."

"Time's coming soon," said Mason complacently, rubbing his protuberant belly.

"Yeah, that's right!" said Marty, encouraging them. "A good war will give all us good guys a chance to clean up a lot of acts. Lot of acts to clean up," he said, shaking his head. "Bust a few heads."

"More than a few heads," said Mason. His eyes squinted hard. "Take more'n that. Got to finish the job that was already started."

"Get the commies left in 'Nam!" Maybe Marty wasn't handling his booze as well as usual, Harry thought, not if he was climbing up on *this* bandwagon.

"Not *that* job. The big job. The job that would have stopped the commie threat in the beginning," said Mason.

"What'd'ya mean?" Marty asked, puzzled. He poured out another glass of Chivas.

"The Final Solution," Mason explained in a subdued voice of awe. "Hell, if we hadn't gotten in Hitler's way he would have taken the commies out *and* he would have done away with the whole problem that caused it in the first place—the Jews. Lenin was a Jew. But they covered it up. We were on the wrong side, that's all. Bleeding hearts got in the way and stopped the Germans from

doing their job with Stalin. It was the beginning of the end. If we'd have just let that guy over there do his job we'd all be better off, not having to worry about commies and the Jews and all those other—"

Harry just put a hand on his forehead and waited. He could sense the change in the atmosphere. Like it was a thunderstorm, about to break and pour down hail, and buckets of water, and forked lightning.

"Look," Mason was going on, "the A-rabs don't want to be on the wrong side. They'd like our help against the Khomeini and all. But they're stuck out there with Israel, and we're giving 'em more of this bleeding-heart shit, and going along with those kike-baby-killers."

Harry took his palm away from his forehead and watched.

Marty rose from his seat in one slow fluid motion. He stood, his little blue eyes tiny circles of hatred and anger. He looked small, skinny. But Harry knew that the force contained in those hard muscles more than made up for the lack of bulk.

"My mama's a Jew," he said, almost conversationally. "My daddy's a Jew. Guess that makes me one too."

Mason and Dolan looked up with quick expressions of distaste.

"My name's Applebaum," said Marty. "Even *sounds* Jewish."

Mason and Dolan didn't know it, but Harry did: Marty's grandparents had died in Treblinka.

Marty's arms moved in a whirlwind. A three-round accumulation of glasses flew through the air. Most just tumbled on the thick red carpeting, but two splintered on the top of an adjoining table. All activity and conversation in the room ceased, and slowly all heads turned toward Applebaum.

"I'm a fucking Jew!" he screamed.

Mason, the fat one, stood up and walked away from the table, trying to give the sense that he was offended and had had enough of the Jew Applebaum's stupidity and boorishness. He wiped his mouth as if the liquor Marty had bought him had suddenly gone sour in his mouth.

Marty lifted his chair and broke it across Mason's back.

Mason plowed forward into the next table, smashed across it, and sagged down to the floor. The three men sitting at that table slowly pushed their chairs back out of the way, but they didn't move to help Mason.

Hyperventilating, Marty stared at the man sprawled on the red carpet.

He didn't notice that behind him Jack Dolan had stood up—with a set of brass knuckles on his right hand.

Dolan was moving up on the little guy, still quaking with the insults.

"Nope," said Harry, putting one great hand around Dolan's arm and effectively stopping his progress.

Harry spoke calmly, as if telling the local bum he couldn't spare a quarter toward a bottle of cheap wine. Dolan looked down at Harry and saw the passive, unconcerned face. He leered at him.

"So, *Greek.* Lots of 'em call themselves Greek."

Harry had to think for a minute before he realized that Dolan was trying to insult him by inferring that he, too, was Jewish. Hell, that wasn't an insult so far as Harry was concerned.

Marty turned slowly. Dolan now stood between Applebaum and Harry, still seated.

"Though maybe Greek's a good word for you, seeing how close you two guys are. You know, *Greek,* what they call *pals* that get too close?"

Dolan's plan was evidently to anger Harry so much that the bigger man would loosen his grip on Dolan's arm and let him use those bright metal knuckles on Harry's face. But nothing an asshole like Dolan could say, Harry thought, would anger him that much.

Marty, of course, was another story.

It was bad enough that these two morons had said what they'd said about the Jews, Harry thought, but even to *hint* that Marty and him—

"You fucking creep!" Marty shouted.

Dolan was so intent on Harry, whose bulk made him seem so much more formidable an adversary, that he had made the mistake of dismissing Marty as not worth bothering with. He kept on thinking that until the little man's feet landed sole-first against his head.

The sound that made was like that of a hammer smashing a glass that's been wrapped in cloth.

Blood poured out of Dolan's nose, and when he opened his mouth more blood spilled out onto the carpet.

The men in the bar were silent. Watching.

Another sign that they were pros. No calls for the fight to stop. No protests. No scrambling toward the exit. No calls to security.

Maybe they just wanted to see how far Marty and Harry would go.

Marty would have killed Dolan. That's about how far Marty would have gone. And afterwards, he'd have pissed on the corpse.

Harry wouldn't let him. He let Marty get off a couple of punches to Dolan's belly, and then Dolan let go a strangled scream that suggested to Harry that something inside his body had ruptured.

Spleen maybe. Or his bladder.

"Enough," Harry said quietly. He put a restraining hand on Marty's arm. Marty calmed down almost instantly.

Dolan was vomiting blood and all those expensive drinks onto the carpet. The mixture stank.

Harry pulled out the wad of bills he carried in his back pocket. He peeled off too many one-hundred-dollar notes, and laid them on the table.

"Time to go," he said to Marty, quite matter-of-factly. He neither ignored nor quailed under the stares of every eye in the place. These were men who had seen worse. "I'm still hungry."

Marty pulled up his pants and tucked in his shirt. He looked around the bar, and then down at the two men on the floor. "Tonight, Harry my man, I am eating *kosher. . . .*"

8

"The world's going to shit!"

Beeker was in one of the foulest moods they'd ever witnessed. Rosie and Cowboy exchanged glances. This was going to be trouble. Delilah studied her fingernails—her favorite aid to concentration.

"They're doing it 'cause it's an Indian's land!" He slammed a hand on the counter that separated the living area of his house from the kitchen. "If this was—"

"The land belonged to a foundation that supported cancer research before you bought it," Delilah said. "It had been bequeathed to them by one of the old pure-Anglo families in Shreveport before that. It was the family that sold the pipeline option to Mexotex. It has nothing to do with your being a Cherokee. Part-Cherokee," she corrected, slyly. "They had never even heard of you."

Beeker's eyes burned as he stared straight at Delilah. Part of him was obviously angry at her denying him his righteous anger. Another part was taking in the fact that she had, again, done some groundwork before he'd even had a chance to ask her.

"Okay. Tell me. Come on. Tell me!" Beeker slammed the counter again. Cowboy and Rosie flinched.

Delilah continued studying her nails. "There's only one way to break the option," she said. "You could buy Mexotex and dismantle the entire operation—"

"I'll do it!" vowed Beeker.

"Fine," said Delilah. "I'll help you take out loans. You and the rest of the boys will be signing out on merc missions for the rest of your years to pay it off, however. I should also point out that in order to keep that pipeline off your land, you'd be raising home heating costs in New England by approximately twenty percent over the next five years. At the same time you'd be putting three thousand Mexicans and fifteen hundred Americans out of work. That would be effective immediately. But, of course, then your hundred acres would still be virgin scrub. It's up to you. . . ."

Beeker turned a darker color. He said nothing.

Delilah stood up and walked over to him. Her body pressed against his, her thighs embracing his legs in that hot way that always diverted his attention. Only when she had established this physical contact did she continue. "It's Tsali too. You're angry about the boy and you're angry about the land as well. The combination is what's getting to you."

Beeker's head nodded a little. "Both together."

"Look, Tsali's going to be fine. I promise you. It's a good school. He's a good kid. It'll work out. You just can't control the land, though. If you wanted to have this much control you should have gone and bought an island. You can still do that."

"No. This is the land I built my first house on. I will stay here. The Cherokee have been marched over half the country and back again. I won't give up."

"Then listen again to what Cowboy's learned. They want to put an oil pipeline through. They own the right to do that. It will be both inconspicuous and unobtrusive. You'll be able to camouflage it. Cowboy's talked to this Cifuentes woman and she's agreed to put it underground if you absorb that part of the cost. You can afford that, without taking out any loans. You can have roads, you can have breaks for game to pass through—all of it."

There was silence. Beeker took a breath and then seemed to relax.

Only the foxy lady could handle this, Rosie thought to himself, glad Delilah was there—and not for the first time. Not for the first time by a long shot.

"Okay. I get all that. But the security!"

"I'll handle it. Promise!" Cowboy had jumped up, daring finally to re-enter the conversation. "Look, I can rewire the security system to accommodate the men that'll be in the area during work hours. I have a promise from Isabella that they'll only work one shift a day, but that that one will be twice the usual manpower. That'll do it in record time, but they'll do it strictly nine-to-five."

"She knows she has the right, but she also knows you can harass her in court," Delilah said. Beeker glanced at her, and she answered his unspoken question. "All you *could* do is harass her. It'd cost her money, but the pipeline would go through."

Beeker sighed again.

"I'll take care of the whole business for you—you won't have to think about it, Billy Leaps." Cowboy spoke a little too gleefully for Beeker's taste.

"Three shifts of guards," Beeker said sternly. "Cowboy, you and Marty are going to pull twelve-hour duty at the consoles. As soon as he gets back you hone him up on how that shit works. Rosie, you, me, and Harry are pulling regular duty on foot, armed at all times, only two half-hour breaks. . . ."

"For Christ's sake!" Rosie objected.

Beeker was adamant. No one argued after his repetition of the orders. He ended: "They're going to violate my land with that goddamn thing. They're not coming anywhere near my house and they're not going to touch one fucking tree they haven't got a right to. That's final. This is supposed to be a fucking military group. Why the hell can't you act like it?"

The military cot in Beeker's room was narrow. It was meant only to sleep a single warrior. When Beeker had bought the stuff for this place he hadn't stopped to consider the niceties of sex.

Now he stood in front of the cot and damned himself. He was angry because Delilah was there, waiting for him—waiting for him in every meaning of the term. Naked, her hands were provocatively exploring herself. That, and they were egging him on, moving against that flesh he had come to desire too much—well, he thought, sometimes too much.

He was naked as well. His readiness for her was as apparent as hers for him. It took all his self-control to stop from just pouncing, just climbing right over on top of her. But he'd learned a lot about Delilah. He knew that neither of them would leave the room before they'd both got what they wanted. The only question was—who would show the greater need? It was a contest Delilah had no intention of losing. She was going to stay right there on the cot and enjoy this. The smile on her face showed that. She enjoyed the subtle mixture of pain and pleasure that this self-denial inflicted on Beeker.

His own hands matched hers as they moved in his private self-exploration. Her mouth opened at the sight, enjoying it, obviously. Her smile deepened. She played games different from those of any other woman Beeker had been to bed with. One more time she was willing to outwait him, match his discipline, equal his quest for control. She moved her legs in a way that added to his need as he watched. He had seen it before but, again, Beeker was struck by the action. It was the kind of thing Delilah could pull, he thought, and it seemed just natural, nothing but natural. On any other female it would have been obscene.

He waited, clenching his jaw to keep from giving in. Beeker didn't like to lose anything to anyone. He wanted Delilah to do it first, to give in, say she needed him. He wanted to hear that before he moved over to her. But the frustration, the waiting, the anticipation all increased until the pain surpassed the pleasure. He moved —no more than a foot. But that foot was enough to give her the victory over him that she craved. Her smile intensified, though apparently she had no need to humiliate him. "Come here, quick," she said. It wasn't an invitation so much as a reward, a little gift to make up for his admission of weakness. If he was angry about it, he didn't show the anger; there were more important things on his mind.

9

Beeker was worried in the morning. He sat at the dining table in nothing but a pair of cammy pants. He was drinking coffee. Rosie and Cowboy both came in, saw him looking blankly into space, and with a look between them, decided not even to say good-morning to the leader while he was in that mood. They poured their coffee and retreated to the security room.

Beeker didn't even look up when Delilah entered the living space. Her perfume announced her. It was the same scent she always wore. It never seemed to increase or decrease in intensity. Though always noticeable, always present, it was never intrusive. She poured her coffee and came and seated herself beside Beeker.

"Not bad. Not that it ever has been." She laughed.

Beeker moved his face to look at her. He said nothing.

Delilah wouldn't give up her smile. "You're the best I've ever had." She meant it. It didn't have to be repeated.

Beeker moved his eyes. He sipped coffee. He put the mug down on the table. "I don't like it."

"Oh?" Her reply wasn't defensive. It was as though she already knew what he was thinking. She was just waiting for him to get the words out.

"Everything's fucked-up. People messing with my land. My boy sent away."

"And me."

Beeker looked down at the table.

"Hard for a man like you, Billy Leaps. You spend all your life

58

building up every barricade a man can construct around his life and his soul. You created a whole self that's based on preservation. It works. It works wonderfully. You had no responsibilities outside yourself. No one to account to. None of those things that most men have to deal with day in and day out. Now, in less than a year, every aspect of that has changed. First you brought back the team. You pulled them all together and you're the leader, the one with the responsibility. No one's giving you orders. No one's giving you advice. Then, fate hands you the son you thought you'd never have. There you are again—making all the decisions, calling all the shots, and finding yourself faced with the same problem all good parents come up against—how to balance what you need with what the boy needs. To cap it all off, along comes a woman who likes you a lot, and you don't care for the fact that you like her a lot in return."

Beeker said nothing. The analysis was correct.

"In one year," she said, "you've gone from having nothing, to having everything. And a pretty sizable fortune to boot, if you were ever really interested in money. You have to remember something, Billy Leaps. Those guys who live here aren't just regular guys. Tsali's no regular son, and I'm no regular lady. We're all pretty special. But then, so are you."

She leaned over to kiss him. A hand ran against his bare chest, teasing him for a brief moment. Only when he sank into the kiss and felt the hand did he also come alive to realize that she was dressed up. "You leaving?" he asked.

"Time to get back to Washington. You're fine. Cowboy's going to deal with the Mexotex woman. Tsali's okay and settled in school. I have a job to attend to—I've got to look out for some more work for the Black Berets, for one thing."

"Yeah, that's fine. I forgot for a minute—you're no regular lady." He couldn't keep the sarcasm out of his voice.

"Forget that one, Beeker. If I were a regular lady and wanted the things a regular lady generally wants, you wouldn't put up with me for two minutes. The last thing you could deal with is a woman living here. I'm no fool, and neither are you."

"Okay, okay." Irritation replaced the sarcasm. Delilah was obviously going to ignore that as well. He dropped the shifting emotions and moved on to business, an arena that he and Delilah seemed to handle as well as they did sex. "Fill me in on the rest of the shit. What's going on here with Mexotex? If I'm going to be dealing with them, I might as well know what there is to know."

He waited. Delilah took her seat again. "Not a whole lot to report, Billy Leaps. I've told you—Mexotex is clean. It's small as pipeline companies go, but that's only as far as pipeline companies are concerned. In its own right, it's a large corporation. It's a little more socially aware than most. The Cifuentes woman really does have an agenda with that phase of her company's business."

"How'd she get to the top?" Beeker asked.

"Her father founded the company a while ago. He used it, originally, to transport natural gas from a field he had struck by himself. It was a prudent move on his part to carry his product to a larger pipeline and to have some control over its distribution. He didn't want to be pushed around by the big multinationals.

"Since then, everything's grown. Grown a lot. The family's made a fortune. They've had good luck with their fields and they made a killing off deregulation. The last field they went after is over the border, in Mexico. It's a killer field. Huge. They're going to become much, much bigger. They don't just want to own the hook-up on this one, they want the whole thing.

"They had the capital and easy credit from some Boston banks so they've decided to use this line to skip over all the Texas-based operations and carry their fuel directly from Mexico to markets in the Northeast.

"Lots of people are going to benefit. Boston banks get the interest on the loans. People in the Northeast stand to lower their fuel costs. Mexicans get to keep ownership of their natural resources. Almost everyone's happy."

"Almost?" It wasn't a question so much as a coaxing. There was more to the story, Beeker knew. There always was on an operation this size. Petroleum and natural gas, more than any other commodity, invited and fostered complexity.

"There's a lot involved here, Beeker. A whole lot. Tens of millions now, potentially a great deal more. But it's nothing to the big boys. They're not going to lose cash money, maybe just have some future markets decreased. The Mexotex operation is a spit in the bucket in this country's fuel needs. But there are some very, very greedy people out there. Some of them are so greedy that the fact that their corporate headquarters happen to be in the United States means nothing to them. They think they're empires unto themselves. There are a dozen corporations, in Texas alone, with budgets greater than the GNP of the Netherlands.

"Word is that one of them in particular, Ranger Petroleum, has gone further than the rest in that kind of thinking. Smart multinationals like IBM make believe there's competition. You'd be surprised how far some of those companies have gone—secretly helping out their competitors—just to make it look as though they weren't functional monopolies.

"Others are too stupid to see the wisdom in that. Ranger's one of those. I don't know what they're up to. But I do know that Washington has some people who wouldn't be upset if they were knocked down a peg or two. Or three or four."

Delilah stood and went to the stove to pour more coffee. She brought back the pot and filled Beeker's mug as well. He was studying her. "You know," he said, "I always have to wonder about you . . . who you work for. Whether you're here for me or as part of your job. Where your information comes from. Why it's always so good. How you already know everything and I just have to come up with the questions you've been expecting all along."

She didn't smile this time. "I told you, Beeker, I'm no regular lady. You're no regular guy. And neither of us has a regular job."

"Yeah, that's true." But the smile on his face wasn't particularly happy. It wasn't satisfied. He was still wrestling with questions about who was playing with whom. Who had the power here? The only thing he felt certain of was that he wasn't going to discover the answers to those questions. Not for a long time. If ever. "I'll drive you to the airport," he said.

10

Cowboy was sitting on the long blue sofa at the end of Isabella Cifuentes's posh trailer. Goddamn, he thought, when that woman said she liked to oversee her company's operations personally, she wasn't kidding. It was a nice trailer—it was the nicest trailer that Cowboy had ever been in or heard about—but the woman, who was probably very rich, was plunked right out there in the cleared path of the Mexotex pipeline. Not the sort of place top oil executives usually spent their weekdays.

She was getting dressed at the other end of the trailer. Cowboy was early for their afternoon appointment—the fact was, he hadn't been able to keep away. He was wearing his darkest pair of sunglasses. That was a good thing, otherwise Isabella would see the lust and longing even more quickly than she'd be able to sense it.

Sometimes Cowboy wondered just what it was about Latin ladies that did him in. The charge was so powerful and overwhelming that he wondered if it wasn't chemical. It wasn't just that he got excited, though he certainly did that. If the woman paid any attention to him, if she gave him so much as the time of day, then another powerful urge came over him. An urge to get married.

Cowboy had done it. He'd done it a dozen times. There were little Mrs. Hatchers all over Latin America. The only thing was that Cowboy hated *being* married. He loved the elaborate courtship. The ceremony. The bridal dinner. The honeymoon. Then he loved getting out.

There was a problem with Isabella Cifuentes and he knew it. He was making believe he was studying the trailer she lived in while he tried desperately hard to figure out that particular hitch. Simply put: Isabella was in the United States. That meant Cowboy had to be extra careful. He'd occasionally made his mistakes too near home, but that had been long ago and he'd learned his painful lessons in alimony payments as a result. No, extra caution was necessary here—extra special caution.

Isabella came in, dressed in a fashion that surprised Cowboy. It was evidently some sort of native costume: bright skirt with alternating bands of vivid color, and a woven blouse of coarse blue material buttoning up the front. Her thick black hair was brushed to fullness then bound with an embroidered band across her forehead. It wasn't at all how Cowboy had expected to see her.

Still, the outfit seemed to fit her beauty particularly well, and Cowboy rose to greet her. He stuck out his hand—one shook hands with oil company presidents, even if they were beautiful Latin women dressed in obscure native costume—but Isabella either didn't notice it, or pretended not to.

Why couldn't this beautiful Mexican woman be in Mexico, where she belonged? That would have made everything so much easier, Cowboy thought while looking at her, drinking in her beauty. It occurred to him then that she was studying him every bit as carefully. Her unabashed attention caused him some discomfort. He tried to get his mind on the business he had with her. Time for the other stuff later.

"So, Señora Isabella, it's all set. It's just the way I told you. You got to cut down a little, let the men work just eight hours, put some of the pipe underground, but no hassle with the courts, no trying to get in your way. Okay?"

She looked up, but only with her eyes. Her head hadn't moved. The resulting gaze was almost menacingly seductive. Cowboy was taken aback by it. He'd never seen that on a Latin woman's face before. She smiled. Now he realized it wasn't that sweet seductive smile of Latin ladies that he loved so much. The smile was like . . . it was like the look Rosie gave women. Increasingly uncomfortable, Cowboy actually felt himself blush.

"You did fine, just fine. I'm proud of you." Isabella Cifuentes spoke as though she were an approving school teacher, not a maiden anticipating conquest. She had gone over to the bar that was set up in the corner of the trailer's living area. She poured herself a glass of tequila. There was enough in the tumbler to awe Cowboy. "Would you like some?"

"Sure, sure," he said.

Isabella poured him a much smaller glass. Cowboy felt pissed off by that. He could drink as much as any woman! he thought. He got even more angry when she proceeded to turn his tequila into a sunrise, as though he had to have the other shit cutting his booze while she was going to drink hers straight.

After she'd mixed the drink and served him, Isabella took Cowboy's hand. The mere touch of her was enough to calm him down, to allow her to lead him over to the couch. She seated him and remained standing in front of him. She took a swig of the tequila then put her glass on the coffee table in front of him. She was smirking now and Cowboy's discomfort returned. There was something wrong with the way this lady was acting. But there was something wonderfully right as well. What was right was the way she was beginning to unbutton her blouse. Cowboy had just assumed that two breasts as perfect and large as hers must have been supported by the most formidable of bras. But only a couple of loosened buttons proved him deliciously wrong. There was nothing but the flawless *chocolat au lait* flesh there. Those things were real and their firmness was natural. He swallowed the saliva that was fast accumulating in his mouth.

"I should tell you about myself, Cowboy." Isabella Cifuentes was smiling, enjoying the obvious response she was getting to the seductive strip-tease she had begun. "I am not from the usual Mexican stock. I come from a very special place."

"Oh?" Cowboy looked up at her. She was shorter than most, but not that much. The way she stood was regal, as though she were of a proud lineage.

"My mother came from Tehuantepec. Have you ever been there? Do you know about it?"

"No." That actually surprised Cowboy, who'd traveled so much in Latin America he thought he must have visited every town with a population over five thousand at least twice.

"It's in the Southeast. It's a very proud place, a very proud people live there. We were never conquered by the Spaniards. The federal government still has a pretty difficult time keeping us under control if there's something we don't like."

She raised her brows and smiled a smile of unalloyed, patriotic pride. "Tehuantepec has the most beautiful women in Mexico."

"I can believe that!" Cowboy was contemplating a lunge toward that valley between her breasts. The skin there was stretched tautly, smoothly.

"We also take a special enjoyment in our men. You see, the women of our region have always been the breadwinners. We rule the family, we rule the marketplace, and we rule our beds."

Cowboy only vaguely heard the words. Isabella had undone another button, even more flesh was exposed, even more of her showed through the opening shirt. Now it was her belly. It was firm. She was going to have a fabulous body, Cowboy thought, just fabulous. Cowboy *knew* it.

But one of Isabella's words had moved into Cowboy's consciousness. One that had stuck out because it seemed so strange. "You rule the *beds?*"

"Interesting, isn't it?" Isabella smiled. "Traditionally we have always held the purse strings of our people. While all the American feminists run around trying to describe the cultural forces that make them think they are so unhappy, we have the actual key. What your women have forgotten—most of them—is that money is the ultimate aphrodisiac. When a class of people has more than another, they not only rule, they get to enjoy the others." She placed a particular emphasis on the word *enjoy* that wasn't lost on Cowboy.

"I laughed all the way through my four years at the University of Texas while I listened to American women. In Tehuantepec my mother's family never dealt with the problems that American females do. Instead we had the privilege of financial control that changes all the rules. We are the ones who whistle at men as they stroll their pretty buns through the marketplace, and we are the

65

ones who make the eyes. Silly American women, if they would just understand the eroticism of the dollar, they could have such a good time.

"Now you, Cowboy, you must understand it. You are having a good time with me, aren't you, blondie?"

"Blondie?" Cowboy was confused. Still trying to focus on her words and not just on the wonders of Isabella's body, he couldn't quite believe the surrealistic story she was telling. "What do you mean?"

"You look at me and you don't just see a beautiful woman, do you? You see a woman with money, power. That's why you are so appreciative, isn't it?"

"No way!" Cowboy started to stand. Isabella pushed him back with an unexpected straight arm.

"Come on, blondie, let's see what you've got."

"What *I've* got!" Cowboy was ready to fight. But the warm hands pulling open his pants weren't doing the kind of thing he really wanted to argue with. It was wrong, he knew, but he let himself give in to her. A moan escaped through his mouth, though he had tried to hold it in.

"Nice," Isabella said appreciatively. "Very nice. Now we'll see the rest."

This is weird, Cowboy thought, *but what the hell? Something new. And she smells so good!*

11

Beeker had come into the living room. He eyed the three other Black Berets there suspiciously. "What the fuck's going on? Who's supposed to be pulling duty right now?"

"Billy Leaps," Harry protested. "Pipeline's still a couple of miles away. Nowhere near your property. We were just having a beer."

"Cowboy's over there right now," said Rosie. "He—"

BAM! BA-BA-BAAAM! BOOOOOOOMMMMMM!

The explosion was powerful enough to rock the house at its foundations. The four men all reacted instinctively. They'd been in too many battles not to recognize the sound of a man-made explosion. They fell to the ground, waiting for any indication that the mammoth detonation would be followed by another, perhaps by one even closer to the house.

Marty stood up before the echo had even died away. "Fucker was less than a mile off." He was swatting the dust off his trousers. Beeker had already begun to crawl toward the ammunition closet. He froze and looked over his shoulder at Marty.

The one thing in the world that the Black Berets could trust Marty Applebaum on absolutely was his knowledge of explosives. If he said it had happened one mile or one hundred miles away, then it had. It was that simple. It was—

"The pipeline!" Harry shouted.

"Let's go!" said Beeker.

The men raced to fulfill Beeker's command. If they trusted Marty for his knowledge of explosives, they had long ago all decided to trust Beeker with even more—the leadership of the group —even if one day they died for their obedience to the Cherokee.

In breakneck time each man had a weapon in his hands. Rosie, Harry, and Beeker had taken M16's from the closet. As usual, Marty broke ranks and was carrying the M60, his favorite weapon. Rosie never had figured out how such a small guy could handle the massive automatic weapon on his own. The black man invariably asked himself that same question at the beginning of every volatile encounter they went into, but there was never time to put the question to Marty directly. After everything was over, Rosie thought, he was always too tired to remember his curiosity, and so he had never found out how Marty managed that motherfucker.

The Jeep station wagon pulled into the Mexotex camp ten minutes later. The confusion caused by the explosion was obvious. No one was still. Over on the northern edge of the site was a crater approximately twenty-five feet wide. Scattered all about was the yellow wreckage of some large construction machine. In a couple of places, Beeker could detect small pools of blood on the excavated surfaces of the land—loss of materiel and personnel, he thought, but how extensive the damage had been was not readily apparent.

Cowboy was okay. He was standing behind Isabella Cifuentes, wearing only his dark glasses and his slacks. The woman herself was screaming a series of orders at her men, one order for anyone who came near enough to hear her.

Rosie ran up to Cowboy. "You okay? You okay, Cowboy?"

The Black Berets were so used to having to talk to Cowboy while he had his shades on that they had learned to read his facial expressions by the lines of his forehead. They almost never got a clean shot of Cowboy's eyes.

What Rosie was seeing now on Cowboy's forehead was utter wonderment. "Man, I thought it was me getting my rocks off." The blond flyer was shaking his head. "Do you believe that?" He pointed at Isabella Cifuentes's back. "That a woman could make you feel that way?"

Rosie slapped Cowboy's bare shoulder and laughed at the flyer's bewilderment. "Way to be, Cowboy," said Rosie softly, "get you *really* excited and we may see 'em drop the big one."

Beeker wasn't in any mood to check out the quality of Cowboy's sex life. He walked right up to Isabella Cifuentes. Not because she was a beautiful woman—those details didn't sink into Beeker's mind at such times as these. He went to her because she was the person in the camp who was obviously in charge. Beeker was attracted to leadership the way Cowboy was to Latin ladies.

"What happened?" he demanded, interrupting the woman's swift flow of orders.

Isabella Cifuentes stopped her rapid speech and looked at the tall half-breed. "Who the hell are you?"

"Beeker. You?"

An eyebrow went up on the woman's brow. "Oh, the big landowner. I'm Isabella Cifuentes. I thought your man said you weren't going to give me any trouble."

"Me? I'm not. What was this?"

"I don't know," she returned acidly. Shaking her head, she surveyed the scene around her. The men seemed to have most things under control. The wail of a siren announced the arrival of two ambulances from one of the suburbs of Shreveport. "Three men injured. One lost an arm. One got his face cut up. And one idiot got a concussion when he ran right smack into a tree. And I lost about two and a half million dollars worth of machinery, plus about eight full days' work."

There was something in her voice that told Beeker that her estimates weren't exaggerated. This was a woman who knew whereof she spoke.

"It was a bomb?" Beeker asked.

"I don't know," she said, "but it sure as hell blew up."

"Who did it?"

"I don't know. Could have been competitors. Could have been you. You didn't want me to build across your land. Bad enough to blow up my camp?" Her voice carried a casual challenge.

"Let me tell you something, lady," Beeker said through clenched teeth. "If my men had wanted to blow your place up,

69

everything would have been blown up. You see that little man over there?"

Beeker pointed at Marty, who was jumping up and down in front of Harry, shouting unintelligibly. Harry, with characteristic placidity, simply listened.

"That man is pissed off because somebody planted explosives within a hundred miles of my farm. That man considers this whole damn county his private preserve. Also considers this a bungled job. The only thing Applebaum hates more than someone poaching on his turf is somebody who doesn't know how to set a charge right. So he's double mad. If I had told Marty to get rid of this construction site, there wouldn't be *anything* left. You and I wouldn't be standing here. Lady, you'd have your tits scattered from Tulsa to Mobile."

Isabella Cifuentes studied Beeker and finally gave him a short nod. "I believe you," she said.

12

Cowboy didn't have much time to worry about his startling sexual escapades with Isabella Cifuentes. The very next day he was standing in a field near Beeker's house and was being swept away by a passion as great as any he'd ever entertained for a woman.

"Beautiful!"

It wasn't a Latin lady this time. It was a helicopter he'd never seen before, only heard about. A single telephone call to Delilah and here it was. The big markings on the side of the craft weren't the most wonderful form of camouflage, but the way the tall letters spelled out the name was equal to the masculinity of the bird: SUPERCOBRA.

"Holy shit."

The helicopter in front of Cowboy was supposed to be only in the planning stages. It was a Bell Helicopter AH-1T. Cowboy climbed into the cockpit and sat at the controls. Marty bustled in the other side and looked questioningly around the enclosed area. "Hell, this isn't a helicopter, this is a computer."

"Oh, man, but what this computer could do!" Cowboy was lost in his own private world, one of fast flying and quick aerial destruction. "What this machine could do. . . ." he whispered.

"How'd she get it?" Cowboy was demanding. But the expression on Beeker's face reminded him that there were questions about Delilah that weren't supposed to be asked. "Okay, okay, I get the message. This whole operation's such a mystery sometimes. If it isn't Delilah coming up with state-of-the-art tinkertoys, it's the goddamned Marines delivering guns in the most barren places on earth, or else some fool handing over a whole cache of arms he's been holding onto for a couple of decades. Okay, okay, I'm not asking any questions."

Cowboy's willingness to let the issue slide had less to do with self-restraint than with his excitement about the typewritten manual for the Supercobra he held in his hands. I want to know *everything* about that fucker, he thought. He'd already spent most of the day with two technicians from the manufacturer, going over the intricacies of the machine. These two—a man and a woman—knew their business. But they didn't ask any questions about the Black Berets and their priority for this secret machine, and they wouldn't answer any questions beyond the field of their expertise.

Cowboy could fly anything. But when he was presented with something this wonderful he wanted to study it in the most minute detail. He didn't want to overlook any of its possibilities through ignorance. He was as bad about flying machines as Marty was about bombs. Sure, each could look at anything within his specialty and make it fly, or blow up, but both men lusted after the details. They had to know just how much more they could pull out of every specific situation they might come up against.

"Come on, Cowboy, enough study time. Get that thing moving." Beeker was staring out the window. It was after nine P.M., and they had decided not to use the machine until it was dark.

"Yo, Beeker. I'm ready to take her up!"

Cowboy was in seventh heaven. The Supercobra moved through the air with a kind of weightless ease. It was like a ride in the first-class section of a 747 after three Scotches. The machine hummed with technical perfection and smelled as fine as a new Cadillac. No other man's sweat had sunk into the seats, no other man's hands had left their mark on the controls. This is how Cowboy liked a bird to be. Virgin. His. As much as possible, his alone.

After a dozen trips, this bird wouldn't be able to get off the ground for anybody else. That's how close Cowboy got to his 'copters.

As the Supercobra swept over the landscape of northeast Louisiana he thought about that. He wondered how he could arrange to build his own. Just start at the beginning of the plant and move up the assembly line, he thought, asking the mechanics how to do this, where to put that, but making sure he did it himself.

What a thought!

He wondered if any of the men at Rolls-Royce ever did that with their handmade cars. Just think what a gas that would be! he mused. Take your own automobile through the whole assembly line all by yourself and know when you drove out that it was *yours*. Yours in a way that almost nothing was in the world today. Something that you had taken from raw material to the finished product. Jesus! A Supercobra that you put together with your own two hands!

The helicopter swept the dark night with its precise movements. Clouds covered the moon and stars. The earth was just a mass of lumpy blackness, now and then punctuated by the beams of a pair of headlamps on a lonely backroad, or the sodium light in the backyard of a remote farmhouse.

No one on the ground, even knowing about the helicopter's presence, would have any fear of being seen in so black a landscape.

But the Supercobra had ways to overcome that. Light? Cowboy thought. Who needed it? Why announce yourself with glaring spotlights that would only show the enemy just where you were? This was state-of-the-art!

Cowboy wasn't peeping out his window to try to find anything on the ground below. Instead he was watching a green screen. It appeared to be the same kind of VDT that he and Tsali used in the security room at the farm. Just a screen, just a scroll of readouts, constantly changing.

But the readouts on this screen weren't computer games.

The screen was attached to a FLIR system. The FLIR—Forward Looking InfraRed—was one of the newest marvels of modern warfare. Its sensitive scanning of the land below could pick up anything living, anything that gave off heat. Just like the security system at the farm which used similar technology to track the possible invasion of Beeker's land by other humans, the FLIR picked up a man-sized body and showed it as a bleep on the screen.

A deer, a bear, any other large animal could set off the FLIR. One of the hassles with the security system on the ground was how frequently a large wandering dog had provoked the maddening siren to go off. Beeker was always complaining about that. But the system also showed when the bodies' movements were the consistent motions of human beings. Those patterns had more than once signified ambushes for the Black Berets and Tsali. The grumblings about getting woken up every once in a while stopped after that was proven.

Cowboy was sweeping the long line of travel of the Mexotex pipeline. He had an accurate report from Isabella Cifuentes telling what quadrants her workers had been confined to. When Cowboy caught something on the screen he only had to check her notes to see if those people ought to be there or not.

What, or who, he was looking for in this night maneuver wasn't clear. Cowboy and the rest of them had tried all day to figure out who would have gone after the Mexotex pipeline.

Physical warfare between companies had been a regular fact of life in the rough and tumble days of the initial oil explorations in Texas, Oklahoma, and Louisiana. More than once the firms had employed private armies to go out and do battle with one another. Now they were too well set-up. They were all getting fat at the expense of the people, through the means of governmental favoritism. The companies' main hopes for success and riches came from their cooperation with one another, and everybody and everything else be damned.

The boardrooms of Houston, Dallas, and Oklahoma City were more inclined to allow an upstart like Mexotex to move in a little bit, plump itself up on easy, initial profits, and then—if its president and board looked deserving of the favor—Mexotex would be brought into the cabal. Then the favors would begin. The subtle price settings arrived at over tall country club drinks. The signals to divide up markets exchanged over dinner. Trade-offs. Buy-ins. Lockouts. All agreed upon so quickly and subtly that a tape recording of the conversation would seem innocuous if not incomprehensible to a jury.

The big oil companies today, some of them the biggest corporations in the world, didn't often resort to physical violence as crass as blowing up Mexotex's pipeline. If they used such means they employed it against their common enemy—the labor unions. Those were heads they'd break. They'd all learned, though, that ultimately the companies were ranged on the same side of the fence.

So who had planted the bomb?

The evidence that Marty had collected from the remains of the explosion suggested that it had been a military job. The bombers had used—misused as far as Marty was concerned—the kind of plastique that would have been pried out of a Claymore, rather than the much more effective and more easily obtained industrial explosives civilians would probably have employed. They'd been amateurs in setting the explosions, so Marty conjectured they'd been out of the service for some time. Or else they were simply following a set of very crude instructions.

Marty had been pissed. Pissed that they'd done it so close to home. And pissed that they'd done it so poorly.

So there was need for extra alertness. They'd all agreed to that. Beeker's demands for security against the oil pipeline people had, in the beginning, seemed an overstatement, a foolish kid's peeved action. It happened sometimes to men like Beeker, but not often enough to get to the rest of the Black Berets.

But they all knew that when you take a warrior like Billy Leaps and put him in a farmhouse day in and day out and then—worst of all—you take away his son, then you cause trouble. Bad trouble. He was like a Marine NCO left in Lejeune while his friends and peers got their platoons blown up in Lebanon. All of a sudden there are unnecessary inspections, unnecessary patrols, unnecessary sentry duties.

If on top of all that you give one of these guys something that bothers him like the explosion bothered Beeker, then the bear starts to roar and the first people he can roar at are his own men.

That's what they'd thought of Beeker's plans at first. But now he seemed to have done exactly the right thing.

The apparently bucolic setting of the Louisiana farm was deceptive. It looked like a nice place in the country outside Shreveport. No big deal. Nothing to worry about. But it was a fortress.

When they had first moved here to join Beeker it was just a piece of land where Beeker had built a house. But that was before they had truly become Black Berets again. The team. Before they'd gone back out into the field. Before they'd begun to act as the most effective fighting group available in the world. Bar none.

Once that had begun to happen and once they had realized that Tsali would be left vulnerable whenever they went out into the field, they knew things would have to change. Sure, there was Beeker's compulsive need to buy land, as if he were going to set up a new Cherokee nation all by himself, with his own checking account. But it was more. They had enemies now. The intelligence networks of the world knew about them—the Black Berets were sure of that.

They were doing things that made a lot of people mad. They were angering the kinds of people who considered vengeance a preventive measure against future attacks. The best way was to get to the base and destroy it, hurt the force by eliminating some of its members—or discourage the force by killing its loved ones.

The Black Berets couldn't let that happen. Now the little one-story farmhouse that had replaced the one that had been torched was a work of art almost as complex as the Supercobra Cowboy was flying. An H-bomb that knocked out Shreveport would blister the outside walls of the house, but wouldn't do much more than that. They knew their arms cache in the ammo room could do for half the small armies of the world, and were convinced the electronic security system would have made the CIA shit—and probably had on more than one occasion.

That explosion, even if it had been meant against Mexotex alone, had threatened the base, threatened the Black Berets themselves. No matter that the first attempt was unprofessional. That wasn't the point. The next time they—whoever they were—could have learned from their initial mistake.

Beeker wasn't into protecting Isabella Cifuentes and Mexotex. He was into protecting the farm. Not for sentimental reasons this time, but because it was necessary for the Berets to have that place. It was necessary for them to make sure that everyone knew it was inviolable. That's what made Beeker get the new 'copter.

The screen was picking up something. Cowboy was brought back to the present. He flipped some switches. There was no need to be foolish. That was the great lesson, he thought. You never underestimate your enemy. Never, ever.

Cowboy circled back around. The screen showed a line of men moving with deliberation. They weren't supposed to be there. He knew that. He checked his notes to be sure. But he wasn't at all surprised when his suspicion was confirmed. He made out at least a dozen men. They weren't campers, because campers don't move through the forest in V-formation. Cowboy moved the Supercobra in closer. An infrared camera was set up in the nose of the helicopter.

Who needs light when you have the most up-to-date technology? he thought. He could operate the camera from the comfort of his leather seat. The photos would be taken back to the farm and he'd find out just what was going on here.

But a sudden burst of light in the deep darkness thwarted his plan.

A missile.

Coming right at the Supercobra.

"Come on, baby," Cowboy grinned.

If anyone had seen the expression on his face as the missile made its way toward the flying machine, he would have sworn that Cowboy had a death wish. An honest-to-God wish to die at the controls. But this was an age of technology pitted against technology —and Cowboy had no intention of going down in flames.

The switch Cowboy threw activated the Supercobra's ALQ-144, an electronically powered omnidirectional jammer. Cowboy was sure the missile would be heat-sensitive, with the kind of minicomputer job that sought out the high temperature of the engine with deadly mechanical aiming power. Because of Cowboy's jamming, the missile started to go crazy as soon as it was launched. So did the second missile. The two deadly weapons traveled off into space —they weren't going to find their target so easily tonight.

Cowboy grinned, leaving the Supercobra in its vulnerable position, as though he hoped they would send up more missiles. But the men below weren't going to play with Cowboy anymore. He gave them a victorious wave and then lifted the powerful machine farther into the air. The helicopter rose with incredible speed. The earth below dropped away into deeper blackness and Cowboy headed home.

He had work to do in the darkroom.

13

Beeker was anxious, as usual. "Come on, hotshot, what the hell's taking you so long?"

But, just as usual, Cowboy was doing his laboratory work with meticulous care.

It was one of the mysteries of the Black Berets that while each of them possessed some adolescent characteristic to a remarkable degree, when each got to his specialty he did it right the first time. Marty and his bombs provided the most obvious example, though hardly the only one. No matter how many fist fights the little blond man got into, no matter how many times he bored the rest of them to tears with his bragging, no matter how obnoxious he was in nearly every social encounter he had, when it came to dealing with explosives, Marty was a consummate professional.

Cowboy might go mooning off after every good-looking Latin woman he found, and he might want to spend the rest of his life snorting the cocaine that Beeker had forbidden him, but when he was at the controls of a helicopter or a plane of any sort he was a textbook case of calm nerves and mature self-possession.

The photo lab was another of Cowboy's babies. Another room turned over to modern science. Beeker would just as soon they all lived in tents wearing nothing but loincloths and war paint. But Cowboy was always finding something new that had to go into the building. The darkroom and the security room, with its bank of computer terminals, were two of the most important to him. Developing infrared film was an extremely delicate proposition. Cowboy wasn't going to let Beeker's impatience hurry him.

When he finally did come out with a stack of still damp 8 × 10 prints, the Black Berets' leader jumped up from his chair and ran over to meet him. "What did you find?"

"I found a whole lot of men walking through the forests with a whole lot of weapons," Cowboy said. The photographic prints were snatched from his hands and the rest of the group gathered around Beeker to see them.

"National Guard on maneuver?" asked Rosie, peering easily over Beeker's right shoulder.

Marty, however, was too short to get the vantage he wanted. "Come on, Beak, put 'em on the table where we all can see 'em."

Billy Leaps didn't pause from flipping through the prints as he followed Marty's suggestion and led the group over to the baronial table that dominated the living space. There he spread out the ten photographs that Cowboy had taken in the Supercobra.

"Not National Guard—a bunch of weirdos." Rosie made his final judgment as he surveyed the different photos more carefully. They depicted the twelve or so men Cowboy had spotted on the FLIR.

The infrared photography process isn't one that can provide sharp pictures, certainly not at the distance the Supercobra was from the ground. The lines were blurred, and the men were walking through a fairly densely wooded area. But the outlines and the shadings that were observable made everything seem clear enough. The men were all uniformed, and were moving in a series of classic military poses. With the utilization of the infrared, Cowboy was actually able to see them loading their missile launcher for the second attack on him.

"What kind of weapon is that?" he asked.

"Can't make it out," Beeker replied. "Could be anything. The details are just too blurry. It's a washout."

"No it's not." Stepping back, Marty crossed his arms and spread his legs. He had a smirk on his face. He knew something the others didn't.

They eyed him suspiciously. Harry spoke first: "What do you see that we don't, Marty?"

"I just see something," Marty replied. He wanted them to ask. It was one of his tricks. Whenever he knew that he had some information that they needed he tried to make sure they begged for it.

"Tell me, Marty," Beeker ordered. He hated all of Applebaum's games.

"Come on, guys," Marty teased, "isn't there something *off* in those pictures?"

They all went back to the table, caught in Marty's ploy. They stared again at the grainy photographs.

"Let's try twenty questions." Marty grinned more broadly.

"We're gonna play twenty Marty Applebaums splashed across the wall if you don't stop this shit and tell us what the fuck you're talking about!" Rosie, obviously, wasn't in the mood to humor him.

The big black man only had to take one step toward the much smaller Applebaum. Marty invariably lost these showdowns with Rosie. "Okay, okay. I'll tell you what's wrong!"

"What!" Rosie screamed, and took another step toward Marty.

"They're fat! They're pigs! When was the last time you saw a whole group of uniformed men who were fat like they were pigs?"

They all turned back to the pictures and studied them again. "Not all of them," Beeker said, "but most. Not fat like pigs either, but overweight. Most of these guys are really out of shape."

The photographs told that truth. The men couldn't be made out clearly because of the distance, but the Black Berets could discern that those forms and torsos belonged to men who were not in training. Not in rigorous training, anyway.

"What does that mean?" Rosie demanded with a snort of disgust. "We're going to discount people who blow up the pipeline because they all need to go on diets?"

"No, it just means we have a good lead on the type of men they are," Harry responded. "They're just like the ones at the convention Marty and I went to. Some kind of survivalist group, some of those play-soldiers who decided to take their play seriously all of a sudden."

Rosie looked over at Harry. "But why? Why here? And why us?"

"If that's who it is," said Beeker. "Could be anybody though. Anybody in uniform. We got to have more information."

"Revenge!" screamed Marty suddenly. "That's who it is, Harry! Those fuckers from New Orleans. 'Cause I punched 'em out! 'Cause I broke their fucking heads! And now they're coming back to get me, and that's why they used explosives, 'cause they knew it would make *me* mad as piss!"

"If they were coming after you," Cowboy pointed out, "they'd have shoved that bomb up your asshole, Marty. They wouldn't have shoved it in the end of the goddamned pipeline."

"Doesn't matter for now *who* they are," said Beeker. "They're armed and they're dangerous. They're also too close. Already fired two missiles at Cowboy and they didn't even know who the fuck he was. That's heavy shit so far as I'm concerned. So till we find out a hell of a lot more, full security stays. Full alert at all times. Cowboy, you get in touch with Cifuentes. I'm gonna have another little talk with Delilah. We got to figure out what all this is pointed at."

Beeker stood at the door of the farmhouse. Waiting, he thought, always fucking waiting. For intelligence, for troops to return, for an enemy attack, for the rain to fall out of the clouds, for the rain to stop falling out of the clouds. Waiting. It seemed the role of the warrior more than any other. Certainly more than any actual combat.

Waiting.

The late spring sun was bright and hot in Louisiana. The farmland that surrounded the house looked good. Good, especially, because it was his. His own. Shared with his men. Land that they could live on for years, for the rest of their lives. Land that his son could inherit.

What else will he get? Beeker asked himself bitterly. A heritage of fighting? Unknown enemies at every turn? Unidentifiable men were combing the area around the Black Berets' home this very moment. And Beeker had no idea what group was after them, nor for what purpose.

82

Beeker had brought the team back together in order to return to Vietnam and search out an old buddy still trapped in a Cong camp. They'd known their mission then, even if it had turned out to be a false one. When they learned that they'd been duped, they went after Parkes, the miserable son-of-a-bitch who'd misled them. Then they had both a mission and an enemy. Later, in subsequent exploits, their goals had been clear-cut and aggressive. They'd taken the offensive against a named, known adversary.

But now? Who was this?

It must have to do with the Cifuentes woman and her goddamn pipeline, Beeker thought, his anger not limited to the desecration of the land now. It was more than that. The fucking pipeline brought this on them. But why? Who was after Mexotex Oil and Gas?

It didn't actually make a whole lot of difference, he decided. Even if he personally didn't give a shit about Isabella Cifuentes, Cowboy did. More, their land and their possessions were targets of whatever group was involved. Or even if they weren't targets, they were near enough to sustain damage.

Whatever the case, the Black Berets were in it for keeps. Beeker kicked the stoop of the stairway with his boot. Seemed like the Black Berets were always in things like this for keeps. Hell, they were in everything for keeps.

Then he relaxed his legs again and began watching in a different direction. Just standing at the door to his farmhouse. Waiting.

14

Rosie at least had something productive to do. The shopping. He loved doing it. Not because the action was anything at all, nor really because he liked the idea of spending half an hour roaming the aisles of the Shreveport Piggly Wiggly. Rosie liked doing it because it was the last thing in the world he would ever have expected of himself.

There he was, the big, bad, mean Viet vet, the man whose knowledge of torture was so ex-human that the Pentagon once sent out some men to 'Nam to study him. They didn't get it all down, he thought. There were parts they left out.

But here he was, standing at the white porcelain counter of a butcher shop in Shreveport's best black neighborhood, arguing with a pretty, *pretty* black woman about a rack of ribs.

They weren't prime, Rosie knew that. But this pretty, pretty lady wanted to charge him as if they were.

Soon Rosie was shouting, and Rosie could shout loud, but the pretty, pretty black lady could shout louder. And did.

Then suddenly Rosie was guffawing.

"What is wrong with you?" the lady behind the counter demanded.

Rosie struggled to regain control of his breath. "Nothing, honey, nothing at all. Just that last time somebody was arguing with me around a rack of ribs—"

"Yeah?" she said.

"—they was *his,* and I was holding 'em, and wouldn't give 'em back. That's what's so funny."

She looked at Rosie, and then grinned, almost despite herself. "I had a brother went over," she said.

"Come back?" Rosie asked.

She shook her head. Then the expression on her face changed suddenly, and after that everything happened so quickly that Rosie only figured it all out later.

First there was a shot and the whisper of a slug alongside Rosie's head.

The shot sent Rosie into automatic pilot. He never even thought about it, but suddenly he was on the cold, gritty linoleum floor of the butcher shop.

Then a louder shot—a shotgun blast.

A soft liquid splash.

A dead man fell into Rosie's vision, collapsing on the floor in front of him.

With a great big hole in his chest, where his prime ribs used to be.

Rosie waited for the screams. You almost always got screams.

Then he remembered. There had been only three people in the butcher shop. Him. The pretty, pretty girl behind the counter. And this white man who came in shortly after Rosie did.

The blood from the white man's wound was trickling toward Rosie. He watched the small stream of blood as it moved. Still liquid from the warmth of the corpse, it congealed as it gathered on the cool tile floor of the butcher shop. Slowly, the line of red fluid moved closer to him.

"Get up off that floor, fool!"

Rosie looked up at the butcher girl standing just beside him.

"You gonna get your clothes all dirty!"

Rosie scrambled to his feet and looked at the small young woman who still cradled a sawed-off shotgun in her arms.

"What the hell—"

"Man pulled a gun on you." She nodded her head toward a pistol that lay on the floor near the cash register. "I saw it coming. Well, we get more'n our share of stick-ups, and we get less'n our

85

share of white men in Caterpillar caps—so I figured *something* was about to come down. I'm always pretty much ready for anything back there."

Rosie glanced down at the dead man. A redneck. Wasn't the type to knock off a butcher shop. Not at all. This one was gunning for Rosie special.

"I told my boss—I said, 'Selma ain't working the shirt off her back to hand over money to some head who's gonna shoot hisself up with poison and starve his babies.' I said to him, 'Get Selma a gun. Get Selma a gun that works!' "

She took one more look at the corpse sprawled on the floor beside them.

"It do work, don't it?" A smile crept across her face.

Rosie imagined a bare-breasted Amazon deep in the African jungle. Returning from a war in which she proved her prowess. Same smile.

"Selma, my name's Rosie. I got to take you out real soon."

Selma looked at Roosevelt Boone hard. She put the shotgun down on the counter. "I guess so. Ain't got no regular man these days. Scared the last one off. Am I gonna scare you off too?"

"I don't scare easy," said Rosie.

"Fine. Now, go on, get out of here, and take your damn ribs too. 'Bout time I called the po-lice, I guess, and not no sense in you being around for that, is there?" she asked cannily.

Rosie shook his head. The Black Berets had no desire to draw the attention of the police—and it looked as if Selma knew how to take care of herself.

"Call you," Rosie promised.

She pointed behind her. "Out the back," she suggested, and that's the way Rosie went.

"Has this whole fucking group gone woman-crazy?" Marty was furious. "First Cowboy goes ga-ga over the spic, then Rosie comes back from town, moaning about some ghetto bunny that he's gotta stick his pecker in before sundown."

"Enough's enough," said Beeker. "Especially when there's stuff to tell us. Come on, Rosie, what happened back there?"

"Okay, okay." Once again, Rosie tried to explain to the rest of them that Selma of the butcher shop was the true embodiment of Afrikete, the warrior queen of Africa.

"Look, what more is there to say? The dude shot at me while I was trying to buy us a rack of ribs. That's all. He only got off one shot 'cause Selma was there with this shotgun and she killed him dead. D-E-A-D. Gun was stolen about three years ago."

"How do you know that?" demanded Beeker.

"Selma figured I might want to know. She's got a cousin—"

"What else did the African queen find out?"

"The police are running the dead man's fingerprints through the FBI files. But there's no ID, nothing on the clothing tags to give us any kind of fit."

"What does that mean?" Beeker demanded.

"Everything this guy had on was from a big chain in Texas. That's all. Lots of people in Shreveport buy their clothes in Texas, it's so close."

"Yeah," said Beeker, "I know that. I also know that this thing is aimed at us. Not just at Mexotex. It was no accident they fired on Cowboy. No accident this guy came after you in Shreveport."

Rosie didn't argue. He knew Beeker was right. Rosie was also quiet because he was ashamed that he had allowed that joker to get off even one shot. Rosie should have pegged him. And just because the other Black Berets didn't throw it in his face didn't mean Rosie hadn't blown it.

"If they know about you," Beeker went on, "then they know about us. If they've done their homework better than they do their fighting, they know about Tsali. I'm bringing him home. Now. Cowboy, get the Beechcraft going. We're flying to New Orleans."

15

"Mr. Beeker, this is most unusual. The Academy isn't accustomed to having students ripped out of its protection with no notice. . . ." Reverend Marchand Delaroche was evidently fishing for an explanation of Billy Leaps's sudden appearance at the school, only a few weeks after Tsali's initial enrollment. "With no reason . . ." He tried again, but Beeker wasn't having any.

"Look, Delaroche, I've come for my son. It's none of your business why."

Delaroche bit at his lower lip. "I, of course, have no legal recourse. There's no way to stop you, though I must advise you against such a course. The boy's life has already been a series of disruptions. This is one more in that painful series."

Cowboy glanced at Billy Leaps. That was getting the man where it hurt. Cowboy saw the Cherokee flinch, but the resolve to take Tsali away was unweakened.

Must be hard on the bastard, Cowboy thought. Beeker wanted the kid safe, of course. But deep down inside, they both knew that Billy Leaps also just wanted the boy home. When it came down to it, Tsali's personal safety was an excuse he could give to get the kid home to Shreveport.

But the question of safety was real. If there was an organized group of armed men out there ballsy enough to attack Rosie in public, Cowboy thought, then they could eventually discover the identity of Beeker's kid and his location in the private school in New Orleans. They'd get him. Tsali'd be an easy target. The kid wouldn't be able to defend himself. Students at the Academy of the Holy Sword probably weren't permitted to go to class armed.

Cowboy wondered if Billy Leaps had considered the thought that chilled the flyer now—if Tsali couldn't stay in school now, when could he? The answer to Cowboy was obvious—never.

The kid was over the line. Past the point of no return. Just sixteen, and no matter what he wanted to do in the future, no matter what choices he might like to make, his destiny was ordained.

He was always going to be a pawn in the hands of the Black Berets, Cowboy thought. He could never just decide, hey, I want to sell insurance and move off to Peoria and forget it all. Never.

Cowboy knew none of them could. But for the men it was different. Each in his own way had decided that this was the way he wanted it to be, this was the way he would choose to live the rest of his life. Cowboy had had options. Cowboy had had experience— too much experience on the streets of the city and on the battlefields of 'Nam. Same went for the others. Each one of them knew what he was getting into.

Tsali had known nothing but loneliness and unhappiness. So he'd found himself a place in the world, a father, some friends, and it felt wonderful to him. But did he really understand that he could never leave it? Cowboy wondered. That while other boys grew up and went off on their own, he would never be able to escape his strange new family?

Cowboy was saddened and depressed by the thought. It was another reminder that he couldn't, shouldn't, ever put a kid into this world. He couldn't, shouldn't, be a father.

He had these thoughts whenever he saw Tsali and Beeker go through something heavy. It was always too heavy for Cowboy, too heavy by half. Hell, Isabella had better be using birth control, he thought. That was a problem with the Latin women, all of them good Catholics. Shit! She could already have gotten herself pregnant.

The door to the office opened and a priest walked in. He was about the same fifty years as the headmaster, and had that same severe, holier-than-thou look about him.

Beeker and Cowboy stood and accepted the introduction to Reverend Artemus George. Delaroche explained the situation. "Mr. Beeker insists that there be no delay. They're taking the boy back with them now."

Reverend George obviously didn't appreciate this. "It's . . . irregular." By his tone of suppressed indignation, it was clear that regularity was something he revered.

Beeker stood impassively, refusing to offer another explanation to a man who was, no matter what else, an underling.

"We have no choice," said Delaroche with a quiet meaningfulness.

"I'll have the boy collect his things." Reverend George turned to Beeker. "The worst thing is the interruption of his discipline. He'll think that you've come to rescue him from his due. Taking him out of the way of punishment now may have severe consequences for the boy's entire future life."

"Discipline?" echoed Beeker, astonished. "Punishment?"

"Tsali has proven to be a very difficult student, unwilling to do things the correct way," said George. "He has had to be chastised . . . more than once. More than twice, in point of fact."

Cowboy couldn't restrain himself. "What are you talking about? Tsali always did everything he was told. And then went back and did it again better."

"Tsali has discipline problems. If you refuse to ignore them, that's your choice as the boy's parent." George pointedly addressed Beeker alone. "It will take a few hours. . . ."

"I want Tsali here in fifteen minutes, ready to leave," said Beeker.

"But the time for packing alone—" Delaroche began.

"Fuck that shit," Beeker said. His only pleasure in the entire interview was the genuine blushes that rose on the smooth-shaven cheeks of Delaroche and George. "Just have Tsali meet us outside. He doesn't have to bring anything with him."

Waiting.
Waiting for enemies. Waiting for his son. Waiting . . .
Finally Beeker could make out Tsali's form moving across the

90

field. A stab of pain pierced his heart. Cowboy's speculations had all been right. Beeker had tortured himself from the beginning about his putting Tsali into this role, this unasked-for, unmerited danger. The kid was so trusting, and Beeker was leading him by the hand—right out onto a mine field.

Now Tsali was coming toward them slowly, more slowly than any other time Beeker could remember. He was probably pissed off to be dragged out of a school like this, Beeker thought. All the fancy equipment, all the friends his own age he could ever want. Then his old man, big-time dad, comes and yanks him away, drags him back to a dirt farm in Shreveport and explains it's all for his own good. Beeker frowned. What a crock that must sound like to the boy.

But when Tsali finally reached the car, Beeker's anger was erased. Something else was wrong, something much different. Tsali wasn't walking slowly out of any hesitation about approaching them. He was obviously in pain. Great physical pain.

The boy wasn't upset about seeing his father, he was desperately relieved. Beeker wasn't deluding himself about that, he was sure. He could see it in Tsali's eyes.

"What is it? What's happened?" Beeker grabbed the kid's shoulders.

Nothing, Tsali signed.

Beeker took a breath and fought the urge to slap the boy for telling a lie. "Tell me what happened." Beeker's voice was low, controlled. Cowboy watched and once again he knew it was a good thing he didn't have a kid himself.

Tsali averted his eyes from Beeker's stare. He seemed to be looking at the ground, as if in shame. But Beeker wouldn't let go of his shoulders. It was clear he intended to stay just like that until he got the story out of his son.

I've failed you.

"How could you fail me? After all the stuff—"

I'm not a good soldier.

"Hell you're not! You're probably the only one here who knows what it's like to be in a battle. To defend your home. To . . ."

Beeker didn't want to think what the boy had been through, already. "Who told you that shit?"

Tsali hesitated again. Billy Leaps struggled once more to keep from shaking the boy into confession. Finally he changed the subject enough to give them both a break. "What took you so long? Were you in a class or something?"

I was being punished.

"What did you do?" Beeker was incredulous. Then he remembered George's nonsense about Tsali being a discipline problem.

I didn't follow orders the way I should have.

"That's a crock of shit." Beeker had lost his patience. After all, he thought, the only really important thing was that Tsali was coming home. "You're good enough for the Black Berets, you're good enough for *anybody*. Come on," he slapped Tsali's shoulder with honest affection. "Let's get out of here."

He led the boy to the rented car that was already being revved up by Cowboy. Tsali climbed in ahead of Beeker and seemed to hesitate. Both the flyer and Billy Leaps watched carefully to see what this was all about. With too much concern Tsali turned to take his seat behind Cowboy. He closed his eyes as he eased himself down.

Tsali had gone through hellish training on the farm. He'd been taught by each of them, driven to run farther and faster, to do more gymnastics, to push his body to the limit. Never in all the trials they'd put him through had the boy ever complained, or allowed the slightest indication of physical discomfort to appear on his face. But when he sat down, finally, there was a silent scream of agony, more hideous because of the boy's inability to create a sound to channel the physical suffering.

Beeker reached in and grabbed the boy. He pulled him forward and out of the car. He stood the kid on the ground again and now demanded, "What did they do to you?"

"You can't go in there!"

Delaroche's secretary yelled the words, but she wasn't about to stand up to the crazed man who burst through the door to the inner office.

The Reverend Marchand Delaroche and the Reverend Artemus George were standing behind the wide mahogany desk. Beeker stalked across the room before either of the priests could regain his composure, move, ask a question—or hide what they held in their hands.

Beeker ripped the photographs from their grasp.

Anger fought with grief, fury battled with sorrow inside Billy Leaps.

"You fucking perverts!"

There, in the pictures he'd taken from them, were scene after scene of Tsali and other teenaged boys, their naked buttocks presented for a clearly identifiable George to apply a cane.

Still other photographs were taken from some secret vantage point. The boys were innocently cavorting in the shower, or changing clothes in the locker room. The photographs of kids who should have been enjoying their adolescence had been turned into a series of sleazy porn photos. These men were daring to take his son, Beeker thought, his son's body, and turn it into something they could go home and jerk off to. Or sell.

Sell!

Beeker's fist flew out and George's jaw crunched under the blow. Teeth spilled out of his mouth along with the blood. Beeker's arm sped through the air and Delaroche went flying across the room. His head connected with the oil portrait entitled "Our Founder."

"The Holy Sword, hunh?" said Beeker, in a low, terrible voice.

He wasn't done with the two men yet.

16

Rosie knelt in front of Harry. They and Marty were already in uniform. Their dressing had been ritualized. Each article of clothing had been put on in precisely the same manner. The knives were attached to the belts at just the same place. The extra ammo was in the same pocket, the first-aid kit secured with precisely the same knots.

The three of them had precisely the same equipment. They knew the reason they had to do it that way: If one of them was dead in the field and another one needed some of that equipment, there wouldn't be time to go searching through blood-stained clothing trying to reconstruct the dead man's idiosyncrasies of suiting-up.

When they were finally dressed in the Black Beret uniforms they both loved and hated, they moved into Rosie's personal ritual. Before every battle the enormous black man went to one of the others to have his skull shaved.

Harry moved the straight-edged razor over the stubbled skin. It didn't matter that the hair had never been allowed to grow long. All of it had to be gone before Rosie would budge. Rosie's head had to be as smoothly surfaced as the tiny ivory skull that dangled from his ear. That earring was Rosie's totem, witness to the hell he had seen in Vietnam. The shaving was the action that moved him, his thoughts, and his soul over the line where citizen was transmuted into warrior.

The Greek thought about this ritual as he pulled the razor carefully and repeatedly across the black man's skull. Putting on the

Black Berets uniform was enough for him. More than enough. That was more transition than he even wanted to think about. But if Rosie needed this other business, then Harry would do it for him. When they were going into the field, Harry knew he'd do anything for Rosie. He had to. Their lives depended on their trusting one another absolutely.

When he was done, Harry wiped off Rosie's head with a towel. The black man stood and nodded in silent thanks. Tsali had been watching. He came over and stood on his toes to rub Rosie's skull. Was it just to feel the newly-shaven skin or to give Rosie luck? The black man didn't know. But he liked the kid's action—and didn't swat away the boy's hand as he would have done with anyone else.

Rosie turned to Beeker. "It would've been easier for you to have just killed the bastards."

Beeker was studying a map at the table. He didn't look up. He knew what Rosie was talking about. "This will be better. They can remember it. They can feel it for a long, long time."

That was the end to the conversation. Rosie clapped a hand on Tsali's back and squeezed his neck. "I would've killed 'em," he said in a low voice to Tsali, and that was the last word that was spoken on the two men down in New Orleans.

"Delilah's information came through," said Beeker. "The men you ran into the other night were on property owned by the Ranger Petroleum Company. It's one of those big multinationals in Dallas. The kind that thinks that American laws are an inconvenience—but not much more than that." Beeker looked around to judge whether his men were properly uniformed. Since he said nothing, the others knew they had passed muster.

Beeker turned back to the map. "We already know that Ranger's been funding some of the groups that you ran into in New Orleans. They do it under the cover of patriotism. Their favorite is something called PAL. It's run by a vet named Jack Dolan—"

"Him," Marty spat out. "He's one of the ones! I told you they were after me for showing them up in that bar, Harry! I told you!"

"Stuff it, Applebaum." Beeker hadn't even looked up from the map. "You three, go in there." Beeker pointed to a sector on the silken surface of the map. "Check them out. I want to know more about whoever's there. Cowboy, we're gonna strap them onto the skids of the chopper. They'll rappel down into this little clearing. Then you stand by. You might have to come in with some air support."

"We won't need any goddamn air support," grumbled Marty.

Beeker finally looked up. "Everybody in 'Nam needed air support eventually, Marty. Cowboy'll be there if you need him."

Louisiana wasn't the tropics. It was warm, even hot in the late spring. It was humid, and every step you took excited a cloud of flying insects out of the forest floor. But it wasn't 'Nam. But this, just this operation, just the transportation in the Supercobra, just the fact they were on maneuvers, was enough like 'Nam to make Harry sick. Sick with the memories.

It was mid-Sunday afternoon. The day was overcast, and the air still. The forest they were tracking through was mostly pine, thick with spindly underbrush that caught and tugged at their uniforms. The floor was thick and mushy with years' deposits of decaying pine needles.

They were moving in a *V* through the underbrush, half a mile from where Cowboy had dropped them. Their faces were mucked with the greasy olive and black paint they had smeared on to block out any possible reflection.

The feel of Rosie's hands on his face had nearly brought Harry to tears. The only time a man ever touched his face was in preparation for battle. The feel of Rosie's thick callused fingers brought it all back to the Greek.

There are some things you don't do unless you intend to follow through on them. When you draw a gun, it's with the intention of firing it. When you put on that uniform and painted your face, you got ready to kill—and you prepared your own soul for death. It didn't make any difference if the battlefield was in Vietnam or Louisiana, the dreadful anticipation was the same.

At the apex of the *V*, Harry was the point man. As usual, the position had been chosen by a flip of the coin. Harry had been the odd man out. The one separated from the others by the luck of the toss. That meant he was most likely to meet the enemy first. Most likely to trip the concealed bomb. To draw the first fire. Or even worse, to get cut off from the squad when the ambushers waited until the whole team was in the killing field.

He'd been here before, of course. Too many times, he thought. It felt the same here in Louisiana as it had in Vietnam. Yet something was off. This was *not* duty in 'Nam. There were never going to be any short days, days waiting to go home. His commitment to Billy Leaps and the Black Berets went beyond that. There was no backing out of it. He was going to spend the rest of his life in preparation for a patrol just like this one.

Harry didn't avoid the obvious fact: the probability there weren't going to be very many of these days for him. Somewhere along the line—

He stopped short. He could sense that Rosie and Marty had frozen with him. No matter how many thoughts had been going through Harry's mind, his trained warrior's mind had registered the alien sound. A human sound. One that didn't belong in this remote corner of the Louisiana pine forest.

Beeker's maps indicated that this large parcel of land belonging to Ranger Petroleum should have been deserted. It was supposedly being held for future development, and was even closed to hunters and campers. There were no buildings, and there should have been no humans. Though, of course, there shouldn't have been missiles flying up at Cowboy's Supercobra either.

Anyone who'd attack an unidentified helicopter wasn't going to hesitate to go after three armed men on the ground.

The Black Berets were already bent over in the torturous crouch of the infantrymen. Now they lowered themselves even closer to the ground. Beeker had taught them that. He'd used the Indian lore to talk to them about merging with the land, working with it to escape the sight and hearing of those whose alienation from the earth made their presence laughingly, and dangerously, obvious.

The Greek, Rosie, and Marty moved a hundred yards in that lowered crouch. They would have been imperceptible to anyone studying the area, but here they didn't need to worry about that. The sounds they had heard before became clearer. The men speaking aloud weren't paying any attention to the forest around them. There was no sentry. *Lousy work,* Harry thought.

They came right up to the clearing where Harry could count fourteen men. Either Cowboy's photographs hadn't picked up the whole bunch, or else more had joined the original group.

It looked, to Harry, like a Boy Scout reunion campout. The men were seated in a circle around a recently extinguished campfire that had been used to cook an afternoon meal. In the middle of the circle was the one man Harry thought he could respect—a man quite different from the others.

He had the stature of the kind of guy who would have been in the SEALs, just like Harry and Marty had been. He was close to six feet, had a military haircut, and while Harry pegged him for forty-five—older than any of the Black Berets—he was in obvious fighting shape.

He stood with the same stance of leadership that Beeker always assumed. The legs slightly apart, the spine stiff, the arms moving with hard chopping motions. No relaxation apparent in his face. He was giving some sort of lesson and was taking it for granted his troops were going to get it right the first time. Harry had his doubts about that.

The talk ended before the three Berets were close enough to make out what it had been about. Instead they got the lecture part of the exercise.

"While Sergeant Mackle's been more than adequate in explaining the mechanics and strategies of organized fighting, let's not forget the motivations that propel men into battle and the convictions that gain them victory."

The man speaking was a lot different from Mackle. His gut hung out over his khaki pants so far, Harry thought, that the only way he could see his prick was if he stood on a mirror. His legs were spindly and seemed incapable of holding up so much weight. Harry watched and listened as the man went on with the usual drivel. A communist conspiracy had entered the mainstream of American life through the agency of Jews and Negroes. Jews were responsible for the decay of the foundations of our country. Negroes threatened our way of life.

Jesus, how do Marty and Rosie listen to this shit all the time? Harry wondered. Then he jerked his head to observe the other two. He trusted Rosie to keep a cool head, but Marty was another story. The sweat beading on Applebaum's forehead was enough to show Harry there was a real possibility of trouble. Marty was actually listening to this garbage—not tuning it out the way he should. Harry's eyes shifted to the M60 cradled in Marty's arms. If Marty blew, so would the whole group in front of them.

"Shut up!" Mackle's voice boomed through the clearing and startled the circled group. He dove for the weapons set in a triangular stack near the edge of the clearing. His rifle swept the forest in the general area of the Black Berets trio.

"What the hell, Mackle—" the fat man was demanding.

"Assholes, there's someone out there. Camouflaged, but out there. This isn't play time. Get your arms. Get to cover."

Harry knew Rosie and Marty wouldn't move. He was in command and the one thing that the Berets, even Applebaum, would always respect was command. He watched the scene unfold.

Only a couple of the "Boy Scouts" were in decent shape, but they had all been trained in at least the rudiments. They all got their M16's and spread out in a *V*-shaped fan around Mackle. The fat man was the only one who hadn't followed his orders. He waddled around in front of the men. "Mackle, this is outrageous, we're not—"

"It's not going to be outrageous if I'm right," Mackle interrupted. "And I am."

Harry appreciated the authority in Mackle's voice. A good man. *Hope he doesn't have to die.*

"Back up slow," Mackle went on. "Keep formation. You, Bosman, get behind me and *stay low.*"

The group dispersed, leaving all their equipment but the essential arms that Mackle had ordered them to take. They moved backwards. Harry decided to let them. He could see the fear on the faces of the men. Their strength was utterly centered on Mackle. Without him, Harry thought, they probably couldn't have fired that rocket at Cowboy's new 'copter.

Harry knew that the entire group would be dead in a matter of a minute or so if he gave the order, but there was no need to have a massacre—except maybe to gratify Marty. No, he thought, he didn't need the whole group. He just needed the leader. Harry figured he'd wait and go for that a little later.

17

It had been as easy as pie to trail the group. Mackle had obviously only been able to maintain the tight military order while the men really did believe they were in danger. The Black Berets understood that any situation in which an enemy might put in an appearance demanded total discipline.

By nightfall, the Boy Scouts' stamina and attention were gone. But the Black Berets remained, concealed in the surrounding forest.

The collection of men under Mackle had a semipermanent base. The small group of huts—evidently buildings that once housed lumbermen—afforded them a sense of safety. That was another sign of the amateur fighter—his willingness to trust in unworthy symbols of security. Home makes a child feel safe, but the child's father understands that a home requires as much protection as it gives—if not actually more.

The Boy Scouts had fallen out by the time the three Black Berets took up their positions around the clearing. They'd gone to drinking beer and laughing with adolescent joy over the sense of danger that had stirred them momentarily. To a man they were convinced it had been an act of training on Mackle's part.

Mackle stood over at the edge of the clearing and smoked a cigarette. Bosman—the fatuous political and administrative leader of the group—had gone up to him and, while Harry watched, the two men obviously had a low-voiced argument. Harry could just imagine the content: Bosman complaining that his speech had been needlessly interrupted, his authority usurped by Mackle's little pointless "enemy" games; Mackle telling Bosman what to do with his speeches and his authority.

A car pulled up into the clearing. It was a big Lincoln. Harry watched as four young white women got out.

Whores.

They were whores, Harry knew, because there was no other reason four such attractive women would pay any attention to this group of men. Harry hoped the young women had been amply paid —for the outrageous flirting, for the wet kissing, for pressing their fine, trim bodies lasciviously against a whole succession of bloated beer paunches and loose flabby thighs.

What kind of operation was this? he wondered. Maybe it *was* a summer camp. March around and play soldier during the day and then have snatch delivered to your bedside. And when you got bored, shoot off a few heat-seeking missiles at whatever was flying overhead. Didn't add up.

The beer was flowing even more swiftly now. Harry ignored that. Instead he watched the other side of the clearing, where Mackle still stood. The pro was as disgusted as Harry was. His body retained the military stance that Harry had so easily identified, and his face was frozen in the earlier scowl. Bosman had abandoned his argument with Mackle and turned his attention to the hired women.

The fat man was running his hand up and down the backside of a redhead pretty enough for Harry to be interested. Or he would have been, he thought, if he hadn't considered the calluses on the girl's mind that allowed her to accept the attentions of a pig like Bosman.

Mackle evidently had the same thought. Harry could see that. But he was watching Mackle for a different reason. The Greek was waiting for something to happen all right, but it had nothing to do with looking on while four women were gradually stripped to bare skin that was pressed against bare earth.

The action was swift, quick, and silent. Rosie's work usually was. Mackle was pulled back into the brush before his unconscious body even hit the ground.

102

If Harry hadn't envied Mackle's position before, he certainly didn't now.

The man was spread-eagled, naked on the forest floor. He was just regaining consciousness. His head moved slowly at first, and his body tried to retreat into a protective posture. But Rosie's bonds kept him wide and defenseless. Then the panic took over. The adrenaline surged. Mackle was immediately aware of every centimeter of his vulnerability.

His head forced itself up off the ground and swiveled around quickly to study his predicament. Probably the first thing he saw, Harry assumed, was Rosie. That would have done it. The shaved head, the demonic grin, and the gleaming skull earring.

Mackle made one more attempt to test the ropes that tied him down. He realized they were secure. His head dropped back against the earth.

"Okay, Rosie, let's go." Harry's command was softly spoken. He didn't like this stuff, not one bit. But there was information to be obtained. It was their job to get it. And Rosie had the best ability to secure it of any man they knew.

"What the hell!" Mackle's head was off the ground again. "What the hell's going on?" His bravado and outrage were an act—testing the ropes again.

Rosie dropped to his knees beside the tied man. "Now, we got some things to ask you and I'm just here to make sure your answers are the ones we want to hear." The black man smiled.

Harry knew that Mackle could see all three of them. They must have looked forbidding, to say the least. Even Marty—cammied up, with his glasses in his pocket—had a certain wiry menace in his stance. If Mackle had been in 'Nam, and Harry somehow was sure he was, then Mackle was certain to sense their status as three men who had been tried, who had come through the battles and the horrors with their bodies and their skills intact. Maybe not their souls. But their bodies and their skills.

"You don't have to do anything but ask." Mackle's voice and statement were crystal clear. "I don't know who you are, I don't think I want to know. But you got shit for me, and there isn't a damn thing I know that I'm not gonna tell you. Just keep your shit for somebody else, will you, fella?" He spoke directly to Rosie.

Harry believed him. Rosie looked at the Greek and saw the nod. Rosie turned back to Mackle. "Who are you?"

"Frank Mackle. USMC, retired. Long time retired. I was a twenty-year-man, but I started when I was eighteen. Been out for ten years. I pick up some extra cash doing survival training, paramilitary stuff."

"Who are they?" said Rosie.

"A bunch of businessmen from Dallas. They're the only thing that stands between America and degradation. In their opinion," he added.

That was a lot of straight-sounding talk to Harry. He motioned again to Rosie. A knife went quickly through the ropes and Mackle was free to sit up. Marty tossed him his clothes. Mackle stood and pulled on his pants. "My boots."

Harry shook his head, no.

Mackle didn't argue, and after a moment's reflection, actually seemed relieved by Harry's refusal. He wasn't getting his boots because he was going to live and be set free. Barefoot, though, he wouldn't make it back to his camp in time to cause these three men any trouble. They'd be long gone before he could mobilize his men, if he wanted to when they were finished with him.

If they had given him back his boots, he would have started to worry about his continued existence on the morrow.

"More information." Harry's statement was as commanding as anything that Mackle had said to the Boy Scouts. Mackle looked up at him with a silent acknowledgment of their equality.

"Look, this guy, Jones—D. Jerrold Jones—has one of those big ranches south of Dallas. He owns this land here too. He's the head of it. He's the one who contacted me." He paused a moment, gathering his thoughts. "I know the smell of money, good money, and he's got so much it could outstink New Jersey. I got signed up with him a few years ago. You know how it is after twenty years—you're used to the life and it's not easy to go back."

They all did know that. They had all tried, and none of them had handled it.

"At first, well, it just seemed harmless. Some of it made sense. You know, the hardline anti-commie stuff. So some middle-aged guys want to be able to handle themselves if the Russkies land? Nothing wrong with that, I figured."

He glanced around at the Black Berets, but neither Harry, Rosie, nor even Marty said anything. They weren't going to get chummy with a man who was still their prisoner.

"So I trained them," Mackle went on. "They're okay, but they're usually only around for weekends. That guy Bosman, though, he's a son-of-a-bitch. Can't stand his type. Scares me a little, I guess. Political types do. I'm ready to leave this outfit. That's one reason I'm talking to you now. These guys are crazy! Or if they're not, the ones organizing 'em are."

He stopped for a moment. No more questions from Harry, but Mackle knew that he was supposed to go on.

"This is one of a lot of groups. It didn't really dawn on me at first how many guys were training, there'd just be lots of them. Some every weekend. And after I did start to count up the numbers, I got another surprise—I wasn't the only one doing it."

Harry and Rosie exchanged glances. They'd seen this part coming. A mile off.

"I met up with a guy in a bar in Dallas. He was in the Corps too. Doing the same thing for the same man. Jones. He already knew another one, another leatherneck doing training for Jones. So there were at least three of us—and maybe more. This guy in the bar— he tried to get out. . . ."

"And?" Harry prompted.

"I haven't heard from him lately," said Mackle. "Not in three months."

Harry looked over at Rosie and Marty. Their faces were expressionless, but the Greek knew what was behind those masks. This was news that Beeker had to have. There was some maniac out there and he was training a fucking *army!*

"Tell us about numbers," Harry said.

Mackle stopped and seemed to be counting in his head. "Twelve to fifteen every weekend. During vacation times, lots more, same numbers, but they come in the weekdays. Return for refresher about once every six months. What you must have seen over there is pretty representative of the shit that's flown out here."

"Well-armed shit," said Harry. "How many altogether?"

"Few thousand," said Mackle. "Me and the other trainers did some raw figuring."

"How well trained?" asked Rosie.

"Lousy." Mackle grinned. "And I do mean lousy. But they can fire an M16, they can fire a LAW, and most of 'em are veterans already, so they got *something*. . . ."

"They can fuck up explosives pretty good," Marty grumbled, his self-discipline cracking at last. But it didn't crack too much—those were the first words he'd spoken in an hour. He was upset that Mackle had turned over all his information without a single nick of Rosie's knife to prompt him.

"I don't know about explosives," said Mackle, shaking his head. "I'm not turning over dynamite to these 'holes. . . ."

"Get going." Harry gestured with the barrel of his M16. "You got a long walk."

"Which way?" Mackle asked.

"Any way you like, friend," Harry responded. "No more favors. Just go."

"No boots?"

Harry shook his head.

When Mackle had wandered off, quickly and without further questions, the Black Berets moved in the opposite direction. A few minutes later, Harry gave Marty a quiet order.

"Get Cowboy down here. We gotta get back to Beeker."

18

It hurt Cowboy's feelings. Really and truly it did. But there was no option. He buckled the safety strap on the first-class seat of the 727 as it stood at the gate of Shreveport International Airport. He hated taking commercial planes. He just hated it.

But then he just thought about the sound of Isabella Cifuentes's voice on the phone and he forgot all his problems with flying, at least for the moment. Then the three jet engines revved up. The problem was that a man who knew as much as Cowboy did about flying just could not believe that anyone else knew how to do it right.

So it was a sophisticated, proven Boeing plane, he mused. So the federal government had god-knows how many agencies insuring safety in the plane and competence in the pilot. So it was an easy hop from Shreveport to Dallas, one that idiot up front had probably made a million and one times. But that idiot in the cockpit wasn't him, he thought, and there was no way he could really know how to fly.

The plane taxied out to the runway and positioned itself for take-off. Cowboy gripped the handles of the seat with the fever of an old woman who'd never flown before and had sworn she never would. Cowboy was *sure* the pilot was going to fuck up. He just knew it. He just—

The engines roared, building up pressure and the speed that sent the big bird hurtling down the runway. Cowboy didn't just close his eyes, he jammed them shut with fear and the desperate belief of the doomed that this couldn't work. There was no way it would work.

He didn't open his eyes until the stewardess was leaning over him. "Would you care for a cocktail, sir?"

Cowboy pried his lids apart and dared to look out the window. The Louisiana ground was far beneath him. The miracle had occurred. Someone besides him had gotten a plane into the air.

"Scotch. A double. A triple." He spoke without looking at her. There hadn't been even a hint of Spanish in her voice, and besides, it was necessary for him to continue to monitor the status of the plane. He was convinced that if he pulled his gaze from the window the wing would fall right off.

She was waiting at the airport.

Cowboy was almost able to forget the psychological torture he had just undergone on the jetliner. His stomach did relax at least a little bit. The sweat stopped pouring from his skin. His heart had something more important to contemplate.

"Hi, Blondie."

Cowboy didn't even react to his nickname this time. She was beautiful. The whole of Latin America reverberated in her voice. She wore the same kind of colorful dress as before, the bright hues of old Mexico mixing perfectly with the unmistakable cut of fashion. He smiled.

Cowboy leaned down and their lips touched. It was all he needed—he was already feeling the familiar constriction in his trousers. The taste of her mouth validated the intense desire he felt when he heard her voice. This kind of passion wasn't supposed to happen north of the Rio Grande, he thought. But in the heat of it all, in the immediacy of her presence, Cowboy wasn't going to argue geography. No way. He didn't want to argue about anything except the location of the nearest motel room.

"We have business to attend to." Isabella turned on her heel and walked away, her initial duty done with that one little kiss. Cowboy followed as though he were a whipped dog, unable to conceive of anything but pacing after his mistress.

It meant that the constriction in his trousers got worse. Because his view now was of her ass, her gorgeous, round, smooth-skinned, voluptuous ass. *Oh my god,* he thought, *I can't look at that!* He stepped quickly to bring himself up beside her. He looked over.

Another mistake. Her fast pace was setting those incredible breasts bouncing up and down. He remembered them from that night in the trailer. They were firm, more so than any he could bring to mind. They stood tall, the nipples pointing almost directly and impossibly upright. He closed his eyes in the memory of them.

And walked into a glass wall.

Isabella Cifuentes was one Latin lady who had never even heard that she was supposed to be poor. She and Cowboy sat in the back of a Lincoln Continental stretch limousine driven by a silent and respectful chauffeur. The driver obviously knew his way around Dallas. Isabella wasn't paying any attention at all to their slow progress through the snarled traffic.

Behind the tinted windows, she was attending to Cowboy's split forehead. "Poor Blondie, to hurt yourself for me."

The pain wasn't so bad, though Cowboy could feel the lump expand. He wasn't going to admit that to Isabella though, not so long as she was willing to play nurse with him. Her cool hands stroked his face with concern. The expression on her face was one that Cowboy knew well, it was one that said he was going to get laid. Amazing, he thought, how much women like to have a chance to take care of men.

Isabella broke off the physical contact and reached forward, flicking a control that exposed a bar built into the seat in front of them. "I'll make you a nice cool drink." A nice cool drink to Isabella was a water glass full of Tequila with a single shot of lime juice in it, all poured over ice from the limo's refrigerator. "Here, my poor Blondie," she said as she handed the glass over to him.

Cowboy closed his eyes with satisfaction as he sipped the beverage. This was the life: the wonderful Isabella Cifuentes close by him, a drink in his hand as the two of them sat in the cool back seat of the limo. This was certainly the life.

Even the luxury of the drive didn't quite prepare Cowboy for the apartment where Isabella lived. It was the penthouse of a large office building downtown. From it Cowboy was given an unmatched view of the cityscape that had become familiar to him from the old days when he had been able to watch television, the days before the imposition of Beeker's puritanical regime. Every week he had watched the opening of *Dallas*. He suddenly felt like Bobby Ewing himself. Sitting here, the entire city at his feet, a gorgeous woman close by, and the sensation of reclining on a great pile of bundled hundred-dollar bills. Well, maybe it was a bit more like being J.R., he thought as he watched Isabella.

She approached him, a lustful smile on her face. "Blondie, your head hurt too much for . . . ?"

"Oh no!" Cowboy answered quickly.

"Good." As happened before, her hands began to undo the buttons of her blouse, the skin came into view, those breasts, that body . . .

"We'll kiss it," she said, "and make it well."

It would have occurred to any man. True, Cowboy thought of marriage whenever he saw a Latin woman as beautiful as Isabella. But any real man would have done the same thing in his current position.

He was under the crisp sheets of Isabella's canopied bed. Exhausted. Absolutely, utterly, completely exhausted. The whole night had been a succession of impossible positions, outrageous demands, and consistent quality. How could Isabella ever expect to find another man who could do all *that* in a night? She was beside him, naked as he was, sitting up with her back against the pillows. The same maid who had discreetly served their breakfast had brought Isabella a stack of newspapers and files.

Any man would have thought about it. *Marriage.*

Cowboy was content simply to study her beauty while she read. He rolled around on the mattress to get a better view. His slight motion caught her attention. "You okay, Blondie?"

"Uh-hunh." He smiled at her. He reached over, though, and grabbed for his sunglasses. He had been conscious for about fifteen minutes now and that was the limit of his tolerance for sunshine, even when it was filtered through curtains. If Isabella thought it was strange that a man would wear his shades in bed with her she didn't say anything. She had already gone back to her reading.

Cowboy idly picked up one of the newspapers and opened it. He scanned the headlines but nothing interested him. He was too concerned with the question of where the wedding should be held. Shreveport, really, he supposed. But Louisiana didn't have the necessary Spanish influence. Nor did Dallas. Perhaps they could rent a resort on the Gulf of Mexico, hire a jet and take the whole group over to Baja. . . .

Isabella slammed down her files and broke his concentration. "Bastards!"

"Hunh?" Cowboy was debating what kind of band should play at the reception.

"I know who's responsible for blowing up the pipeline. I had my suspicions before, but now I know for sure."

"Who?"

"Ranger Petroleum."

"That's what—" He nearly said *That's what Delilah told Beeker.* But nobody was supposed to know about Delilah. "That's what we heard," he finished vaguely.

"It's beginning to make sense. Do you know D. Jerrold Jones?"

"I've heard the name mentioned." Cowboy was holding his cards close to his chest now. Of course he had heard the debriefing that the Greek had made when he came back from the scouting mission. Jones was the man who was paying for the training of the PALs.

"He's always hated me, me and my father. He loathes the idea of any Mexicans at all having money, and the fact that my family made its money out of competition with RP is just about enough to give that tub of lard an apoplectic stroke."

Cowboy marveled—when Isabella was angry, she seemed to lose her Spanish accent altogether. It was in bed with him that it was most pronounced.

"It's here in these documents," Isabella said. "Ranger's investment in northeastern natural gas sales is even higher than I had suspected. Much higher. My pipeline is a direct challenge to him and to his liquidity. I love it!" A kind of grim satisfaction flooded

111

her face. "I could be ruining Ranger Petroleum. I could bring that bigoted motherfucker down all by myself."

"They're pretty big-time for you to ruin them all by yourself," said Cowboy cautiously.

"Even a corporation as big as Ranger can overextend itself," said Isabella. "Look at Continental Illinois—one of the biggest banks in the world and they nearly went under because of the volatile energy market and a series of stupid investments. Maybe, just maybe, Ranger Petroleum has done the same thing. If they're as far out on that limb as I think they are, Blondie, my pipeline is going to snap that branch. And down will come baby, cradle and all. *Splat.*"

Isabella looked down at Cowboy. "Just thinking about winning against Jones makes my blood hot, Blondie. Very hot." Her hands explored beneath the sheets and quickly found their goal. Cowboy thought it would be impossible, after last night. But her palm found his center and the massage began, so gentle, so delicious. "Come on, Blondie, I need you." Her hand grew more insistent. "Come on, for me, please." Her mouth was next to his ear now. Her breath was hot. The hand moved so smoothly that the impossible happened. Isabella Cifuentes took immediate advantage.

She moved herself on top of him and now it wasn't just her breath that was hot against Cowboy. There was something else hot and wet and wonderful pressing against him. He felt a brief stab of pain, last night had . . . But he forgot that as he was enveloped in her and as she began that rhythmic series of movements that he had learned to love. He sprawled out on the cool sheets, letting her breasts rock against his chest as she moved. His mouth came up and sucked in one of her dark nipples, already fully erect. She threw her head back at the contact. She rode him, she rode her cowboy, hard and quick, with long slippery motions. In only a few moments her cries of pulsating release echoed through the room.

How he had ever found the energy to join her orgasm was beyond him. It seemed as though she had pulled it from his very belly, her tight, strong muscles actually *demanding* that he come. So he did.

They were both exhausted again. She kissed him gently on the cheek. "Thank you, Blondie. Money and power do that to me," she added, with a sort of sublime innocence.

Then it was she, and not Blondie behind his shades, who rolled over and went to sleep again.

It definitely should be a mariachi band. Cowboy had decided that much. And Baja sounded just fine. Isabella was still dozing when a second maid quietly brought in another tray with hot chocolate. It seemed a luxurious second course for the morning meal. After that little encounter, Cowboy needed something smooth and easy. He sipped the sweet drink. It was delicious. The milky texture slid down his throat.

Life was good. That was all there was to it, he thought. Life was good. He could feel Isabella's cool hip against his own. He looked over at her as he sipped his chocolate. He felt wonderful. Sleepy. As well he should have. Cowboy wondered how long a man could expect to survive as the mate of Isabella Cifuentes. It was the first time he had ever even contemplated sticking around that long with a Latin wife. It was the last thought he had before he passed out from the drug that had been placed in the hot chocolate.

19

Cowboy felt a familiar sensation. Even behind a blindfold and with his hands tied securely behind his back, there was no doubt about it. He was in a helicopter.

He couldn't for the moment discern anything else. Not the time of day, the reason for his capture, or the identity of his captors. The 'copter was moving fast, that was the one thing he could figure out. He also knew that Isabella was nearby. He could smell her. Or maybe it was just her lingering odor on his body from the night before.

Cowboy moved just a little bit to test his bonds. Someone was watching for him to make just that movement. "He's awake." There was some movement in the 'copter. It must be a big machine, he concluded, because there was no problem with balancing the load. Cowboy felt hands behind his head and then the blindfold was whipped off.

If Cowboy had had daydreams about J. R. Ewing earlier, now he thought he'd woken up in the middle of a Saturday morning cartoon show. In front of him was a man who was the final caricature of a Texas tycoon.

He was wearing a white suit over a white shirt. His string tie was clasped with a turquoise rock at his neck. Correction, he thought, make that a turquoise *boulder*. His white Stetson was curled up absurdly high on both sides of his head, and the rift in the crown was as deep as a Texas gorge. The man had an enormous paunch. Enormous! His stomach was a study in the cantilevered suspension

114

of weight. He swooped far out from his midsection, as though he were shoplifting watermelons. Someplace underneath that mound the man must have a pecker, Cowboy thought. And maybe he'd see it someday if he used a periscope turned upside down.

To top off the image, he was smoking a cigar. Your five-dollar type that could stink out an Olympic stadium. His thumbs tugged at his suspenders. He was staring down at Cowboy with a thoughtful expression on his vast, fat, sunburned face. Then his gaze shifted to Isabella. "Get her up." He spat the words out of a mouth that seemed absurdly tiny and precise for a man of his massive, obese bulk.

A stooge moved quickly and tore the blindfold from Isabella's head. He grabbed her hair and slapped her soundly. Once. Twice. On the third blow Isabella came awake with an uncharacteristic little girl's cry. It made Cowboy all the more angry and all the more intent on throwing out vengeance in every direction, like a dog shaking off water. No one handled one of Cowboy's women that way. Even if it was Isabella, who always before had been able to take care of herself.

The fat man studied Isabella. She was naked now. The blanket that had covered her had been removed during the awakening.

"Spic slit makes me wanna puke my guts."

His words matched his body, thought Cowboy.

"You put your thing in that?" the fat man demanded of Cowboy. "You're gonna rot from the middle toward both ends."

Cowboy lurched as far forward as his bonds would allow. He spat at the fat man. But the Texan's stooge wasn't tied up at all, and Cowboy took a thudding boot-blow to the chest. He crashed back against the hard metallic wall of the 'copter.

A third man ran up to Fat Texas and whispered in his ear. Fat Texas nodded. "Time for work. Double check them two."

The two stooges quickly and silently made sure that Isabella and Cowboy were securely fastened. They placed the bound pair side by side and then tied them together for good measure. Their naked bodies touched from shoulder to ankle when they were done. One of the men obviously didn't share Fat Texas's disdain for Latin women. He ran a hand roughly over one of Isabella's naked breasts. She tried to bite him, which only prompted him to tweak her nipple with rough mirth.

"Bastard!" Isabella screamed in frustration.

"Didn't know your maid was working for me, did you?" Fat Texas said, and grinned.

Cowboy knew he'd remember these faces for the rest of his life. For their wives' sakes, he hoped the stooges' insurance was paid up.

There was movement. Others came forward and Cowboy could now see that there were at least six men besides the pilot in this cargo helicopter. He checked out the craft and saw that it was a fully armed gunboat. Bolted to the floor at each of the open cargo doors was Marty's darling—the deadly M60.

Cowboy'd seen outfits like this in 'Nam. What the hell was it doing in Texas? he wondered.

Settling his bulk carefully into a seat that had evidently been constructed just for him, Fat Texas took the gun nearest to them.

"Jones," Isabella whispered quickly.

D. Jerrold Jones.

The 'copter dived. The familiar drop in altitude registered in Cowboy's stomach. A gleam came over Jones's eyes, the tiny beads buried deep in the flesh of his cheeks lighting up with excitement. Then the other familiar sound reverberated through Cowboy's head. The sound of a machine gun sending deadly fire through the air. Cowboy apologized to Isabella and then painfully forced both of them off the floor of the 'copter enough for him to look out the small window.

Down below, in the dusk light, Cowboy saw a broad and slow-moving river, low sparse vegetation, and a long running fence whose metal links here and there caught the gleam of the helicopter's search light. Cowboy also saw several dozen men and women.

Running hard.

It was easy to put the observations together.

The terrified running figures were wetbacks, starving Mexicans desperate for a chance in life, and the only way they'd ever get it was to cross the Rio Grande into the United States. But from the remaining sunset glow Cowboy knew that the 'copter was forcing them north—*toward* the U.S.

Didn't make any sense.

Then Cowboy saw the break in the fence—a large, deliberate break. And he saw what the wetbacks couldn't see—behind a cover of large bushes men were calmly waiting for them. With weapons.

The 'copter was herding the wetbacks like a shepherd's dog.

Jones's bullets were the dog's bark. And just plain old Texas fun for Jones.

The pilot was obviously well versed in the expected maneuvers— the copter veered sharply. Jones let out a rebel yell of excitement and shot off the machine gun once more, its deadly sounds easily heard over the roar of the 'copter rotaries.

What the hell? Then Cowboy saw.

Down below, a running woman tripped on the uneven ground. She pitched forward face-first onto the earth, and the child she had been carrying flew forward a few more feet.

A line of M60 bullets tore across both prone bodies.

The mother and child danced and bled in the fading afternoon light.

Cowboy continued to strain to look out the window at the ground below. There were more of the stick figures being herded north, toward the break in the fence. Cowboy could tell when the wetbacks saw the apparent hole to freedom, for their speed picked up and their movements were even more frantic. Once all the figures had proceeded through the gap in the fence, the helicopter soared and veered once more, and landed on the American side.

The pilot bounced the machine only once, but Cowboy lost all respect for him.

With surprising agility, Jones hopped down out through the cargo bay.

Bumpity, bumpity Cowboy imagined his belly bouncing on impact. Saturday morning cartoons again.

The other men followed Fat Texas Jones.

Cowboy had hoped that this would be his and Isabella's chance to escape, but the Texas group returned before Cowboy could accomplish anything beyond a severe bruising of his wrists. Evidently

117

Jones's group already on the ground had done their work quickly and efficiently.

D. Jerrold Jones was hoisted back in through the cargo bay, then one of his henchmen herded in a dozen males aged between fifteen and twenty-five. On their faces was shock, nothing but the deepest shock and despair.

Tears ran down their cheeks.

Their break for freedom had failed. They obviously thought that Jones and his men were border guards. They were all handcuffed behind their backs and meekly followed the orders of the captors, shouted in absurdly-accented pidgin Spanish.

The rotor revved up again. The noise was overwhelming. Isabella was jammed next to one of the new prisoners, who was too upset even to take note of her nakedness. She talked to the man in quick words over the noise of the 'copter. Cowboy couldn't make out their conversation, but after a few moments, Isabella whispered to him, in a stricken voice, "They only took the men. The young men. They're afraid the others are going to be killed. The old men. The women. The children. Dozens of them. Cowboy, what's going on?"

Cowboy had no answer.

20

The 'copter landed on a farm at least an hour north of the Rio Grande. The armed men quickly and efficiently gathered up the Mexican captives and with unrestrained use of their rifle butts herded them off toward a barn and other outbuildings not far from the landing spot. Cowboy and Isabella were obviously going to receive some personal attention from D. Jerrold Jones.

At the fat man's nod they were loosened from the helicopter wall and a blanket was thrown around their shoulders. They were untied to an extent that allowed them to walk together, side by side. They were led out of the 'copter, and the waddling rotund figure of Jones led them toward the main house.

It was back to television time. The house was an oversized replica of Tara. Its pillared porch rose dizzyingly into the sky, and the first-floor windows alone were at least fourteen feet high. The white walls of the house gleamed from the flood lights theatrically placed on all sides of the building.

With an armed guard on either side of them, Cowboy and Isabella walked through the main door of the house and into the ornate receiving room to their left. It was obvious that Jones had turned a decorator loose on the place, and not restrained the man in terms of budget. Everything was gold—gold-colored carpets, gold paper on the walls, paintings in wide gilded frames, gilded chandeliers, yellow upholstery on all the furniture. It wasn't the sort of place to be comfortable in, and it was a little too cold and studied to be intimidating. Conspicuously out of place among all the splendor was a dark-brown vinyl Barcalounger, evidently the chair reserved for Jones himself. Probably nothing else in the room would support his weight.

Jones was already seated in his creaking recliner, his chewed cigar replaced with a fresh one, a tall glass of iced drink in his hand, his smile broad and self-satisfied. "What you saw out there, Hatcher, was a bold and daring strike for the American way of life."

Isabella and Cowboy remained silent.

"The constant influx of your foreign types into our fine country has weakened the fiber of our national fabric, Hatcher. It has degraded our bloodlines, and through irreligious intermarriage, we have been in danger of turning the U.S. of A. into a kennel—a *kennel*, Mr. Hatcher, of nonproductive, sap-licking *mongrels.*"

Despite the rhetoric of half-remembered phrases and imagery, the sincerity of Jones's voice made it clear he believed every word he spoke. Cowboy had heard the same tone before, when CIA men talked about the Vietnamese. Instead of describing them accurately as skilled men who were fighting for their homeland, they were presented as subhumans. It was supposed to make it easier for the American troops to kill the enemy. What it did was to make it very easy for the average American soldier to underestimate the courage, the prowess, and the willingness to fight of the average Cong soldier.

"Since the government of the U.S. of A. is *already* in the hands of the communists and the communist-loving liberals, the country no longer has the willingness, or even the ability, to defend itself against this pernicious onslaught from the godless, verminous south." He looked at Isabella meaningfully. "That's why, Mr. Hatcher, I have taken it upon myself to do the work the government itself should have been doing all along."

Isabella couldn't hold her tongue any longer. "By killing women and children?"

"When you want to rid your house of vermin," Jones said without hesitation, "you first go after the ones that are gonna breed like vermin. Ain't that logical now? Eliminate one breeding female and you not only get rid of her but you've canceled out her children

120

that were gonna come along, and her children's children, and finally—a hundred years on down the line—you've wiped out a whole goddamn continent of spics—just by slicing open one goddamn worthless spic slit."

Fat Texas ruminated for a moment, as if he considered this a question of genuine philosophical interest. "See, Mr. Hatcher, the reason for putting a bullet between the eyes of a man, is so that down the line he won't put a bullet between *your* eyes. But a bullet for a man's just not as . . . *economical* as a bullet for a lady." He smiled at Isabella. "A bullet in a man's brain kills the man, a bullet in a woman's brain kills her and her offspring for every single generation that's to come. I'm not only protecting myself, I'm protecting my two boys, and all my grandchildren. I'm insuring the quality of their lives in the year two thousand and ten."

Cowboy fought to hold himself in check. Isabella was going to blow, that was obvious. As much as he wanted to tell this fat slob off, Cowboy figured he had to use even more self-control to balance her emotional state.

"You're sick, Jones. *Sick!*"

"You're wrong," he returned mildly. "I'm just looking at this whole goddamn problem in a straightforward way. That's all. I'm the one who's really got the thing figured out."

"Why are we here?" asked Cowboy. "You got a reason for everything else—you must have a reason for that."

Jones smiled. Cowboy didn't like his smile either. "It sure looked to me as though you two might be going to breed some mongrels. Infringing on my grandchildren's natural rights."

"You bastard," Isabella shot back.

Jones smiled grimly. "I've seen you before," he said. "In Dallas, putting on the airs like you was lily-white. Made me want to puke my guts. That was in a restaurant, and I said to the management, 'Get rid of that spic clit before I puke my guts,' but they wouldn't do it. So I just left, and next day I *bought* that goddamn restaurant, and I shut that fucker down."

Isabella's face drained of the emotion she'd been holding in. Probably, Cowboy surmised, because she now realized she wasn't dealing with a normal, rational human being with a set of entrenched and reactionary beliefs—she was dealing with a madman.

Jones seemed disappointed that he wasn't going to get any more lip from Isabella. He ashed his cigar on an ornate tray next to his comfortable chair and went back to the original question. "Why you, Mr. Hatcher? You had to be taken care of. You and your veteran buddies from Shreveport had begun to make problems for me. For my plans. Mexotex by itself was bad enough—but Mexotex with your men behind it . . ." He shrugged. "I don't like interference, and I decided it would be better to get rid of you now, before you did me any real damage. Besides, the thought of you two together . . ."

Isabella and Cowboy exchanged glances—they were still naked beneath the blanket they shared over their shoulders. Both were filthy and bruised and weary with anxiety. And in one another's eyes they saw concern and fear for the other's safety.

Jones struggled to his feet. "Now, it's my bedtime. I hope you'll excuse me. My men have plans for you, Isabella. They've never seen you in a Paris gown, and I haven't told them that you are president of Mexotex. Without your fine clothes, and your limousine, and your nameplate, you're another Mexican whore, and I could make a guess that's how they're gonna treat you. You've already expressed your interest in white cock," Jones said, glancing at Cowboy. "Well, tonight I imagine you'll get your fill. In every hole you got in your whole goddamn body."

Isabella said nothing. Beneath the cover of the blanket, Cowboy squeezed her hand, helplessly.

"And you, flyboy, let me tell you something. The racial heritage you were born with was the finest gift God set on your ugly head. The finest. But any white man that would stoop to living with Indians and niggers and then bedding a spic cunt has given up the right to that heritage. You like Mexican pussy? Then you live like you're swinging a Mexican prick."

He smiled, then signaled to a guard at the door.

Isabella and Cowboy were taken away.

Separately.

The blanket went with Cowboy back outside. Isabella was led naked deeper into the house.

21

Cowboy was in a fury. He was dressed now, sort of. They had given him a loose-fitting pair of pants belted with a thin string. But he was still tied. This time to other men—about a hundred of them in fact. A long stretch of chain ran down the walls of the crude wooden building where he had been taken. Attached at regular intervals to the chain were Mexican men, including most of those who had been picked up by the helicopter in the early evening.

Everyone got a filthy pallet to sleep on. The manacles attached to each man's right ankle meant that you slept on your back or didn't sleep at all.

In that large, foul room, some men snored, others wept audibly, others prayed in low murmuring voices, still others—near enough for Cowboy to see—merely lay with their dry eyes wide and staring.

Neither sleep nor sorrow came to Cowboy. Just anger, anger and the knowledge that he and the Berets were going to get Jones. It never occurred to him that Beeker and the rest wouldn't save him. The Black Berets hadn't lost just because he had been stupid enough to get captured.

The thought of Isabella nurtured Cowboy's anger, acting like a bellows on the flame of his drive for revenge. That a fat slob like Jonoo would have taken that beautiful Mexican lady and handed her over to his goons . . .

Damn it, Cowboy thought, I'm going to get him.

And carve off a little of that fat.

Somehow, sleep did claim Cowboy that night. He was awakened with the rest of the men by a loud, shouting group of white men, all better dressed than the ragged Mexicans in the hut. They were walking the lines of sleeping figures and beating the soles of their feet with hard painful blows of a long stick.

"Up, up you lazy bastards!"

Cowboy had decided that his first objective was to figure out the terrain. He had to find out what this place was about, how it was laid out. Just because he was chained in the middle of a line of a hundred men didn't mean he had lost his responsibility as a reconnoiterer. And that meant, at least for the time being, that he wasn't going to fight back.

He followed the line of chain as the men walked out of the building into the blinding sunlight. Shit, he wished they hadn't taken away his shades! The prisoners, even those who had only just been captured, were already defeated. Cowboy figured it must have been from sheer ignorance. What guy, grown up in a village in the backwaters of Mexico, would question that this was the way it happened when you tried to cross into America? he thought. This might as well be any prison in the world to these defeated peasants. When would they have heard about penal reform or due process? They had taken their one big chance to become Americans—even if only illegal ones—and all they knew now was that they had lost. That they had lost big was just one more piece of the bad luck by which their entire lives had been governed.

After each man in the line had squatted for a few minutes over the narrow trench that served as latrine, they were all marched through a food line. Tin plates without utensils were given, one to each man. A bored, slovenly cook in filthy kitchen whites ladled a lukewarm gruel onto the plates as each man walked past. A tin cup of bitter coffee was handed to each man. Then, when the line had been served, the men, obviously used to this treatment, simply sat on the ground, the sun already hot on their necks. They ate with their fingers, licking the surplus off. There weren't going to be any linen napkins in this alfresco mess hall—Cowboy saw that soon enough. Also, there wasn't going to be much, not if these guys

125

were going to go so far as to clean their hands and their plates with their tongues—giving up even that shred of dignity.

Cowboy studied the men on either side of him. On the left was an older guy. He at least looked older. He also looked utterly defeated, the way some of the old men had looked in 'Nam, the ones for whom death, war, failure of crops, and homelessness had been such a constant that the concepts of peace, plenty, and contentment were as distant and unearthly as heaven itself. But on Cowboy's right was a much younger man. He looked barely older than Tsali.

Without even looking in the teenager's direction, Cowboy began to speak in Spanish. "How long have you been here?"

"Quiet," the youngster answered, speaking into his bowl of gruel. Smart kid, he didn't look at Cowboy, and no one glancing at them would have known that the boy had spoken. "They get mean if they think you talk too much." Then, after a slight pause, when his eyes quickly scanned the location of the guards, he continued. "A year, give or take. I'm not sure. Longer than some, not as long as most."

"How did you get here?"

The boy gazed into his bowl. "My wife and me, we were crossing the river. Then helicopters came. We thought they were immigration people. They shot at us. They killed my wife. Then armed guards captured me."

"What goes on here?"

"Work. Work and more work when that work is done. We are slaves."

Cowboy ran a finger through the remnants of his gruel, trying to decide whether C-rations were worse, or marginally preferable. "Slaves?"

The young man didn't speak, he only nodded. "We're digging irrigation channels. I doubt if we'll ever finish with them—there is so much land here. Not so long as I live." He laughed shortly, as if to say, *And who knows how long* that *will be?*

One of the guards walked by. Cowboy looked up at him. He was tall, the same six feet as Beeker, and looking almost as powerful. He was also mean, meaner than hell. He wore khaki pants and a matching short-sleeved shirt open at the neck. He wore a bush hat and, tied around his waist like a belt, a long cat-tailed whip. The handle dangled from his left side and whished as he walked. By the way the Mexicans looked up at the sound, Cowboy knew it had become both familiar and dreaded. The guard grinned down at Cowboy, then spoke over his shoulder to another guard. "Looks like some Yankee daddy got himself a piece of Mexican pussy. I ain't never seen such blond hair and such white skin on one of these guys."

The guard evidently hadn't expected Cowboy to understand or to be able to speak English, for he whipped around when Cowboy replied quietly, "My mama and daddy were Texans. My mama was from Galveston, and my daddy was born in Amarillo."

"Who the fuck are you?" the guard demanded.

Cowboy shrugged. "Name's Cowboy."

"I don't give a fuck what your name is, what the fuck are you doing here is what I want to know."

"Ask your boss," said Cowboy. "What are *you* doing here?"

The second guard gestured impatiently to the first. "Come on, Seeley. Let's get this fucker in gear."

"Yeah, okay," the guard named Seeley said, still staring at Cowboy. Then, in a loud voice, "Okay, amigos, vamos." He yanked the whip with a single great tug and its long, ugly length came to rest on the ground. The look on the face of the old man next to him told Cowboy that it wasn't just the *idea* of the whip that frightened him. The old man had suffered beneath those cat-tail lashes in reality.

Cowboy had spent long hours in the sun before. He'd paid out-landish amounts of money to fly to Hawaii, to the Bahamas, to Aruba—all of it just to get into the sun. He'd rested his nearly naked body along the length of a comfortable pool chair and broiled there with a tall gin-and-tonic in his hand.

It wasn't going to cost him a cent to get this tan.

The Texas sun was torturous. Cowboy felt his skin crisp from the prolonged and unremitting exposure. Standing beside Manuel, the young Mexican he had talked to during breakfast, Cowboy knew there was no way to protect himself from the burning rays. The guards kept marching by, never allowing the men a moment's rest. The loose trousers barely reached Cowboy's knees. He could even feel his calves burning. The tops of his bare feet were certainly getting the worst of it.

They were digging a deep irrigation ditch, about four miles from the main house, as nearly as Cowboy could estimate. Two other hundred-man teams were working on parallel ditches on either side of them, fifty yards distant. Over to the west, Cowboy could see lush groves of fruit trees where the ditches like these had already been excavated. They'd probably dig the ditch, then they'd plant the trees, then later—if any of them were left alive—they'd probably pick the fruit.

Manuel had described the endless hours of this digging. He told Cowboy he had survived the boredom and the repetition by praying to the god of the Catholics. Not for himself. He felt he was beyond hope, beyond redemption. He prayed for the soul of his murdered wife.

"Don't you want to get even?" Cowboy asked at one point.

Manuel, who had carried on the entire conversation without lifting his eyes from the earth, suddenly stopped moving and raised his eyes to Cowboy's. "It is hard, sir, to have hope when your body is held by steel."

They continued digging. Sweat dripped down Cowboy's body, a steady rivulet of it coming from each of his armpits and another from his groin. The wetness of his skin only served to hold the prairie dust. It soon caked him from head to foot, and though it was uncomfortable, it protected him to some small extent from the damage that the sun might otherwise have inflicted on his pale skin.

Only when at least a quarter of the men had been lashed for throwing aside their tools in exhaustion was the digging line instructed to cease work. When the order was delivered in Spanish so wretched that it made even Cowboy wince, one hundred men sagged against the earth.

There was no shade. Not at midday. Not this far south in Texas. There was no food either. Cowboy understood now why the men had been so anxious to clean those breakfast plates. A young boy raced up the line with an enormous tray and allowed each man a tin cup of favored water. After him came another boy with a second tray, collecting the emptied cups.

"There's vitamins in that."

Cowboy peered up at Seeley, who had suddenly appeared between him and the sun.

"What do you want? A commendation from the Red Cross?"

The two men glared at one another. It was Seeley who broke the silence. "I know you. Why?"

Cowboy shrugged.

"Hey, Seeley, get over here!" someone called.

The guard left, but once more glanced at Cowboy over his shoulder.

22

Beeker paced the main room of the house. Tsali watched him. His father was not to be trifled with when he was in one of these moods. The boy had never really tested Beeker; he'd never wanted to, never had any reason to. But he understood that there was a core to the big half-breed Cherokee that should never be touched, not even by those he loved.

The phone rang and Beeker nearly ran to it. He spoke in monosyllables. Somehow Tsali knew it was Delilah on the other end of the phone. When he was done he slammed down the receiver and stared at it. "*Shit!*" was all he said. Then he turned to Tsali. "Get the others."

"We're going to Dallas," Beeker said without preamble. Rosie, Marty, and Harry sat in a semicircle at the table with Tsali.

"Dallas?" Harry asked. As usual, there was no emotion in his voice.

"Dallas. Cowboy may be in trouble. Cowboy probably is in trouble. There's more happening with the Mexotex deal than we knew about. That and the other company, Ranger, that we heard about. Dirty, dangerous pool."

"Dallas." Harry repeated the word with the same lack of emotion, but this time there was agreement and affirmation in his voice.

"Man, I bet there are some foxy ladies in Dallas," Marty began. "You think that Isabella Whatever-the-fuck-her-name-is was hot shit, you just wait to see what I'm gonna airlift out of there."

"This is a mission," said Beeker. "There's already too much pussy mixed up in this already. Those PAL guys you came across in the woods are all getting together, and we don't know what for."

"Let me guess," said Rosie.

"And there's a report that Isabella Cifuentes is on honeymoon in Venezuela with her new husband," said Beeker. "Señor Sherwood Hatcher," he added impassively.

Rosie wouldn't buy it. "Cowboy would've invited us to the wedding." He meant that Cowboy would never leave the Berets without warning or explanation—not even for a Latin lady of such attainments as the president of Mexotex.

"Dallas," Harry repeated. This time the word meant, *Let's go.*

She hadn't told him that she'd be there. Still, Beeker wasn't surprised.

"Nice flight?" she asked.

"Better when Cowboy's up front. Trust it more."

That was it for small talk. Delilah and the Black Berets rode to the Hyatt in silence. They were stared at in the lobby. A woman who looked like *that,* entering the exclusive penthouse elevator with four men . . .

But all the speculations of the guests and the hotel personnel didn't get at the truth. Once inside the penthouse suite living room, Delilah was all business, and Beeker, for one, didn't like the lines on her brow. He suspected that this thing—that started out with a clause on a land deed that he had failed to read—was getting bigger all the time.

And Beeker was right.

"D. Jerrold Jones is the chairman and president and founder and principal stockholder of Ranger Petroleum," Delilah began abruptly. "Pictures and files over there. The company's headquartered here in Dallas, but Jones runs the operation from down here." She pointed far south, toward the Mexican border, on the large and full detailed map that had been spread on the conference table.

"This ranch—it's called the Triple-Bar-D—is the second largest in Texas. Bigger than Rhode Island."

131

"Frontage on the Rio Grande," said Harry, studying the map.

Delilah nodded. Expressionlessly she said, "We've recently discovered that Mr. Jones uses illegal aliens as target practice. The women and children at any rate."

"Great," said Rosie, looking at the photographs of Jones. "What does he do? Sit on 'em?"

"I'm sorry to say," said Delilah, "that when Mr. Jones is not shooting the innocent from his helicopter, he is making plans for a major disruption of the world economy."

No one said anything. Delilah went on.

"It's complicated. It involves Middle Eastern politics, it involves a very subtle manipulation of the world's spot markets for petroleum, and it also involves Mexotex Petroleum and Pipeline. When Jones puts his plan into operation it will make the oil shortage of '73 look like an empty shelf at the corner grocery."

"He wants to make a killing," said Marty.

Delilah shook her head.

"No," she said, "he and his friends in Libya, and his friends in Iran, are after something else—a total disruption of the First World economies. They have a three-prong plan. First: drive up the price of oil in America. This is complicated in itself, but to put it simply, within the year we'll be paying three-fifty a gallon for gasoline, and nearly that much for heating oil. Second: to flood one of the NATO alliance countries with so much oil that they drown in it, while drying up the sources for all the others. A glut in Italy, for instance, while France and Germany and the Benelux countries have nothing. And third, to *pour* money into one or more of the marginally stable Third World countries—Mexico, for instance, or Argentina."

"What would that do?" Rosie asked.

"Those countries have lived with debt so long that the whole country would probably collapse around the new prosperity." They all looked skeptical, and Delilah shrugged impatiently. "I'd give you a brief course in macro-economics, but that's not the real issue. The point is that Jones, in league with his Middle Eastern friends, is perfectly capable of causing a series of worldwide economic disruptions that will make the Great Depression look like a bounced check."

"He got a reason for wanting to do this?" Rosie asked. "Or is it just kicks?"

"No," said Delilah. "He's got one big reason. Jones is intensely patriotic. And he thinks that the country is going to the dogs. He thinks that the only way to save the country is to destroy it. If he wanted, he could probably find a way to precipitate a nuclear war —but in the long run that would be detrimental to real estate interests. So he's decided to cripple the country—and the rest of the free world—economically. So that when it learns to walk again, it'll be in step with his own ideas. His own ideas are basically racist. For the past twenty years, Jones has singlehandedly supported a laboratory in Idaho whose only purpose is to develop a racially-selective nerve gas."

Marty grinned. "He's not gonna like us butting in. A Jew, a half-breed Cherokee, and a black man. Hey, Harry, maybe he'll let you live."

"Not Harry," returned Delilah seriously. "Harry's south of the Alps. Greeks aren't blond enough."

"What does PAL have to do with all this?" asked Beeker, who found paramilitary training in the forests of Louisiana of more intrinsic interest than international oil cartels.

"Diversion," said Delilah. "To take people's minds off rising oil prices, and to give the government something to occupy itself with while Jones does what he wants to—PAL intends to precipitate a few major race riots."

"Christ," breathed Rosie in disgust.

"Anti-black riots in Newark, Atlanta, and Richmond. Anti-Jewish riots in Chicago and Boston. Anti-Chinese riots in Seattle and San Francisco. Anti-Spanish riots in Miami and Manhattan. That about cover the bases?"

"Can I kill him?" asked Marty suddenly. "Can I do it? Harry, if you get there first, will you hold off till I get there?"

"Any ideas on how we might get at him?" Beeker asked.

Delilah shook her head. "Field strategy always was my weak point."

133

"Fine," said Beeker. "Glad there's something you're leaving up to us. Anything else you need?" he concluded with a trace of sarcasm in his voice.

"Just one thing," returned Delilah. "Bring Cowboy out safe."

The first day in the ditches had been hell for Cowboy. His skin was burnt raw, especially his neck, which had been bent and exposed to the sun, and the tops of his feet, where the skin had always been covered with lizard- or python-skin boots. He ached all the way back to the camp.

Another meal of sorts was waiting for them there—an over-cooked and soggy mixture of rice, green vegetables, and beans. Now Cowboy didn't just have to speculate on what made the Mexican laborers eat all their crumbs, he knew. He was famished.

When they were done with this scanty supper, they were herded back into the same shack where they had slept the night before. Exhausted, they fell against the wall, and then slumped down onto their pallets. Some began snoring as soon as they hit the ground.

Cowboy talked softly to Manuel. "We got to get out of here."

"Sometimes," the Mexican responded mysteriously, "we get taken out."

Cowboy would have asked Manuel what he meant, but at that moment Seeley moved toward them. He didn't stop to speak, but he tossed something at Cowboy. The flyer, sensing some taboo being broken, hid the small item. Only when Seeley had passed by did he pick it up and examine it.

A candy bar, already unwrapped. So that Cowboy wouldn't have to hide the evidence of the wrapper.

Best present the man could possibly have brought.

Calories and energy in the chocolate and sugar. Protein in the nuts. A sense of well-being at the very luxury of the tiny thing.

Cowboy broke the bar in two and slipped half of it into Manuel's hand.

"We got a friend," said Cowboy.

"Why?" asked Manuel, who had no reason to trust guards, especially not the one who wielded the cat-tail whip.

"I don't know why," Cowboy replied. "Just be glad we got one in this god-forsaken hole."

That night, when Cowboy was asleep, the old man on the other side of him disappeared.

In the morning, Seeley took up the slack in the chain.

"Where is the old man?" Cowboy asked.

Seeley pretended he didn't hear.

"Sometimes," Manuel said again, "we get taken out."

Now Cowboy understood what he meant. The old man just wasn't useful any more. His work didn't equal the pitiful amount of food he'd been given.

Seeley found Cowboy in the trenches again that afternoon, shortly after the midday break.

" 'Nam," said Seeley. "Cavalry."

Cowboy didn't look up. He still didn't remember Seeley, but there wasn't any point in saying that. "You got it," he said, as if he'd known it all along.

"At Da Nang?" Seeley asked.

"Every fucking day."

"Shit," said the guard.

"Yep."

Seeley then screamed at Cowboy in his terrible Spanish—that justified his lingering presence to the other guards.

"How'd you get yourself into this?" Seeley asked then, in English.

"Same question to you," said Cowboy, never losing rhythm with his shovel.

"It's a job."

"The job you got?" said Cowboy contemptuously. "Not for a man."

That was a risk. A big risk. But Cowboy had to push Seeley to see what he was made of.

"I got my reasons," said Seeley. "At Da Nang, did you know that Indian guy? One that got his ear shot off?"

"Beeker," said Cowboy.

"Hey, yeah," said Seeley. "I forgot his name." He took a swipe at one of the Mexicans with his whip. Just to show he was minding the store, Cowboy guessed.

"I owe that fucker."

"You a jarhead?" Cowboy asked. He still hadn't looked up out of the ditch at the guard. Just kept on shoveling and talking in a low voice out of the side of his mouth. And feeling his neck burn.

"Was," said Seeley. "Got a dishonorable."

"Didn't know they gave 'em to jarheads. Thought the good stuff seeped into your blood and sloshed around and never came out again."

"Sometimes that's what it felt like. But something happened . . . and I ended up here."

"You want to pay Beeker back?"

"Hunh?"

Cowboy put down his shovel. Wiped his brow. Looked Seeley in the eye.

"You wanna pay Billy Leaps Beeker back for saving your worthless life?"

"It's not my life. Like I say, I owe him, but it's not for my life— you can believe that."

That night, though he would have preferred to go to sleep for about three years, Cowboy talked to Manuel. About Mexico, a country Cowboy knew well. A country Cowboy loved. He described the mountains in Chihuahua, where Manuel had grown up. A hard place, of course, but every hard place has its beauty, especially if you were born there. Especially if you had never known any other place.

The nostalgia hit the kid pretty hard. Cowboy mined it. He wanted the boy's mind on that, the thing that still existed, the place he could get back to. Cowboy didn't talk about the boy's wife—probably she had been even younger than he was—because his wife was dead, and Manuel could never go back to her.

Seeley came by with another candy bar. Manuel turned on his side, away from the guard with the whip.

"These'll rot your teeth," said Cowboy, giving the boy half.

Next morning it poured rain. That made the gruel thinner but it improved the flavor of the coffee. It kept most of the guards in their Landrovers, and it allowed Seeley, who had volunteered to patrol the three lines of workers alone, to talk at length with Cowboy.

"Tell you something, Seeley," Cowboy said. "Beeker's gonna find me. He always has, he always will. You got to be ready. And you got to get me ready."

"There's no way in hell he's going to get in here. The place is a fortress. This fucking ranch takes up three counties almost. And the whole thing's surrounded by electrified fence and every inch is patrolled. No one, but *no one* is getting in here."

"Then you don't remember Beeker that well. It must not have been a big deal, him saving your fucking worthless life, Seeley. What'd he do? Cull some twelve-year-old sniper out of a bamboo outhouse?"

"More than that," Seeley said, with sudden awe in his voice. "It was a fucking miracle."

"Well," Cowboy said, "whatever it was he did, he's gonna pull another fucking miracle. If I were you, I'd want to put myself on the side of the angels. And the angel that's gonna come out on top here at the Triple-Bar-D is a half-breed Cherokee with half an ear that the devil himself bit off in a barroom brawl."

"There's no way I can get you out of here," said Seeley, unease in his voice, and in his eyes as well.

"You don't have to. You just have to get some information for me. Information that will get us ready when the time comes."

Seeley hesitated. "What do you want to know?"

"I want to know where Isabella Cifuentes is. I don't want to have to waste time searching for her. That, and I want a detailed

138

description of Jones's layout. When Beeker gets here, I want to know where the planes are, where the rifles are, where the explosives are. Hey, you ever hear of a guy named Applebaum?"

Cowboy saw Seeley's shoulders contract when he mentioned the name.

"Oh yeah," the guard whispered, *"crazy* motherfucker . . ."

"Applebaum's coming too," said Cowboy. "So just remember your training. Fucking jarheads—you always do. Just think about it that way. You're getting called up, is all. The biggest leatherneck of them all is on his way and he's going to pass judgment at your inspection. You're just gonna have to be ready."

You had to talk to Marines that way. Cowboy hated it. He hated them. They were all over the fucking place. All over the world. It was true, once those bastards went through basic training you simply could not erase what had happened to them. Each and every one was the same. Say the magic words and sing the right anthem, and they beat each other up to see who gets to throw himself on the first grenade. Cowboy'd caught Seeley. All the years in between, and that dishonorable discharge, didn't mean shit, he thought.

Cowboy was sure that when Beeker did show up, Seeley would salute, turn on a point, and start shooting at Jones's goons. Being a Marine was more important than anything else in life to these assholes, he concluded. They never forgot.

"You'll have it all," Seeley said, and went off with a smart crack of his whip.

Afterward, Cowboy was sorry he hadn't ordered up a pitcher of margaritas, for him and Manuel.

Fucking Marines.

24

The four Black Berets were already advancing along the perimeter of the Triple-Bar-D ranch. In their uniforms, costumes that displayed their souls darkened by war, their faces painted, Rosie's head shaven, they were doing the first work of the warrior—investigating the enemy stronghold.

They worked in silence, each man fully aware of his job. The entire section they could see was lined with steel mesh. Atop it was not just barbed wire, but wire that was woven from razor-sharp strips of metal. Its deadly weave jutted out from the rest of the fence at a forty-five-degree angle, assuring that any fool who attempted to climb over it would shred his skin as easily and quickly as spuds were attacked by an army private. Occasionally there was another deadly warning: THIS FENCE ELECTRIFIED.

There was no indication how much electricity flowed through the steel fence, but judging from Jones's reputation, the charge was probably greater than whatever was allowed by law. Enough to knock unconscious a grown man in the best of physical shape. Enough to kill practically anyone else.

The plains of Texas at this point were flat, flat as the earth can be. The horizon was miles away, and even in the moonlight, scarcely visible. Between that line and the Black Berets there wasn't the slightest hint of roll in the land, just its never-ending sameness. That held one advantage: there would be no ambush. It also held the opposite disadvantage: there would be no cover.

Knowing that the moonlight was sufficient to allow them to see any foe, the Black Berets were able to run and not concern themselves with the slight noise of their boots crunching on dry earth. In a four-wheel-drive vehicle they had arrived at a location far from the road that approached the minor eastern gate of the Triple-Bar-D. Leaving the small truck in a clump of sagebrush, they'd hiked a full six miles—not only to speed their arrival, but to accustom themselves to the feel of the terrain.

Up ahead, like a beacon, was a single bright light. It shone, as they had expected, at the guard house to the Jones ranch side entrance. They were looking for some answers, and the first clue was going to be right here.

As they approached the light they slowed, and became even quieter. When they came within two hundred yards of it they went into their most intense mindset, the one where they left behind their humanity and became a single engine of war, the team of deadly killers that had been fashioned and forged in Vietnam. On their stomachs they moved across the arid soil.

It was different from 'Nam. It wasn't insects and jungle rot that blinded them and stifled their senses, it was dry, fine dust. Not monkeys chattering in trees and wild pigs rooting in the dense foliage, but only the leathery flapping of ground-dwelling bats disturbed by their passing.

Their carefully cradled M16's led the way. As in the jungle, because some things never change, they forgot their discomfort. In battle, in the midst of an action, you don't worry about sores, abrasions, pains, cramps, punctures, or bites. Those things didn't matter when bare survival to the next morning was the real issue.

So Rosie knew he couldn't take the time to fix his shirt, to cover the naked area that was being scraped bloody by the small rocks and pebbles of the desert. And if the dust was aggravating Marty's asthma, he wasn't going to pick this moment to complain. Harry? Pain, of one kind or another, was a given in the life of the melancholy Greek. He'd learned to accommodate it long ago. The pain that Harry felt wasn't going to be materially increased by a scraped knee, or a little mouthful of coarse desert sand, or the sting of some obstreperous beetle. A long time ago Harry had learned that pain was part of his life.

If Beeker was uncomfortable, well, he'd never have admitted it anyway—not even to himself—so no one worried about that.

As they crept towards the guardhouse, Beeker was in the lead, the other three behind him in a vague diamond formation—Rosie to the right, Harry to the left, Marty bringing up the rear. When Beeker stopped moving, the rest froze automatically.

They were within earshot and sight of the guardhouse now. It was small, like an outhouse, or a tollbooth on a bridge nobody wanted to cross. It could hold a couple of men if both of them stood up all the time. A phone of some kind was obvious through the window, and if there were alarm switches they were all well out of sight. Two men were standing outside the post, smoking cigarettes and talking in a way that suggested they'd had this conversation not once but many times before.

"Damn, it's only two o'clock and I'm already out of my gourd."

"Ames," the other guard answered, "you are as lazy as a Mississippi nigger. You get a decent job and all you do—"

"I ain't lazy," Ames protested. "Just bored. I mean, twelve hours a shift—"

"Yeah," returned his companion. "Well, you just tell Jones you want to form a union so you can get paid for doing eight hours of nothing instead of twelve hours of nothing."

"That's the problem," said Ames. "For twelve hours it's goddamn nothing. Nobody comes through. You don't speak to a goddamn soul. You don't see a goddamn thing. And once a night the goddamn alarm goes off because some fucking coyote has just got fried on the fence. If they're gonna bring in everything by 'copter why the fuck do they need three fucking gates?"

"Mr. D. Jerrold Jones has got two billion dollars in his checking account. You know what you can do with two billion dollars?"

"What?"

"Anything you damn well please."

The Black Berets lay still, breathing Texas dust.

Beeker watched it all. He lifted his head an inch out of the dirt. Harry and Rosie didn't need any more signal than that.

They crept forward, scuttling over the desert floor with no more noise or notice than a spider.

The two uniformed Black Berets got within a few yards of the guardhouse and the two men showed no sign of breaking off their unfriendly, rambling conversation. Beeker noted their M16's carefully placed beside them.

Rosie and Harry were both big men. Awfully strong big men. They let out a cry—a cry from each of their throats that was so well synchronized that they seemed to shout with one stereophonic voice. The cry served its purpose. It froze the two guards in momentary shock. Out of desert silence came noise. Out of desert blackness came two camouflaged men. Out of boredom came sudden blows that dropped the guards quickly into unconsciousness.

They woke with their hands securely fastened behind their backs. A thermos of ice water found in the guard house had revived them and soaked their clothes. "What the hell?" exclaimed the man named Ames, shaking his head like a soaked dog. Then the pain hit him, right in the back of the neck. He moaned and collapsed back onto the dry earth that had quickly soaked in the poured water.

"Got some questions for you." Rosie was smiling. His earring was the only thing white he wore—a small white skull that seemed obscene against his dark skin. "Your head hurts a little now. You give me trouble by not answering my questions nice and fast, I'm gonna make it hurt a little more. And then I'm gonna make you hurt in a few other places too." Rosie's white teeth flashed in the moonlight, reflecting the same way his earring did.

"Not much to tell," Ames said in a shaking voice. No fight in this one.

"I ain't gonna tell you jerks a thing!" the other yelled, as though to make up for Ames's lack of spine.

Rosie picked up on the feistiness in the other man's voice. He left Ames and walked over to him. The other guard was evidently Ames's slight superior. His glowering face stared defiantly up at Rosie. The Black Beret reared back and sent one of his huge hands smashing against the captive's cheek. "I think you got *lots* to tell this Mississippi nigger."

The blow had crushed the man's nose. Blood, mucus, and unwilling tears of pain flowed down his face. Rosie bent over and, ignoring the man's screams, placed a finger on the broken nose and waggled the shattered cartilage. Each slight motion wracked the man with renewed and increasing agony.

"Lots," Rosie repeated ominously.

There is no man who can withstand torture. None. Even the best trained and most loyal American troops are told not to bother trying to be overheroic once torture has begun. There is no use. You can't withhold the information the enemy wants if he has the skills to extract it from you. Rosie wanted the information. Rosie had the skills. The man should have seen that and stopped his melodramatic and ultimately pointless resistance.

The other extreme exists, of course. Men so terrified of pain they'll spill everything before the first screw is turned. Ames was one of those cowards.

Blood is ugly, real blood from real wounds. The sight of a broken nose is ugly by itself. The ways the senior guard's body was contorting in pain was real and ugly as well. Ames saw that. Ames did not want to be subject to the same experiment.

"I'll tell you," he yelled over to Rosie. "Whatever you want to know."

Rosie went back to Ames. There was no expression on his face, but what he felt was disgust at Ames's lack of backbone, and relief that he wasn't going to have to work any harder this night. Rosie squatted beside the bound figure. He looked up at Beeker.

Mission accomplished, his eyes said.

"What's with these fences?" Billy Leaps asked.

Ames stared at the big Indian. As much cruelty as there was naked on Rosie's face, there was something about this man that made Ames wish he could be talking to the black man instead. But he wasn't going to chance anything. "They're all around the ranch. There are normal fences a hundred feet or so farther in, so the livestock don't get out and get fried."

"Then what are they for?" Beeker demanded.

Ames hung his head, as though he might start giving the Berets trouble. But a slight movement from Rosie convinced him he should keep on talking. "To keep strangers out, to keep the ranch private. And to keep the workers in," he added after a moment.

144

"Workers?" Beeker prompted.

"They got these wetbacks in there, they get 'em when they try to come over the river. Mr. Jones says if they want to work in America that bad, he ain't gonna be the one to stop 'em."

"They ain't even human," grumbled the other guard, his broken nose making his voice sound as if he had a bad cold. "They can't hardly even understand English. Bunch of—"

Roosevelt Boone had very definite opinions about rednecks who considered anyone, other than themselves, to be subhuman. Rosie also had a few choice thoughts about modern-day slavery as well.

He jumped up from Ames and delivered a heavy thumping kick into the man's groin, one so intense that the guard couldn't even scream. His mouth opened in silent agony and shock. His eyes widened to comic dimensions as he stared first at Rosie and then down to the source of the pain that was more than he could ever have imagined.

Rosie's boot had been aimed perfectly. Almost everything physical that Rosie did was perfect. The guard's testicles had been turned to mush by the violence. As the man stared, blood began to seep through the light khaki material. The man's piss—released by his terror—joined it and spread the stain. He passed out, not knowing if his balls would ever function again. They wouldn't.

Rosie returned to Ames. "How many men in there?"

"Th-three hundred," Ames stammered in his eagerness to reply. "Three hundred armed, I mean. About fifty ranch hands. They got guns, but . . ."

"But what?" said Beeker.

"But they're not PALs," said Ames more slowly, trying to gather his thoughts. He didn't want to chance saying something that would displease the black man standing over him. He didn't want to trigger that boot. "Three hundred armed PALs. Fifty regular ranch hands. Kitchen and house staff—that's about twenty. And five hundred wetbacks. That's all. I think that's all. The hands and the aliens—they don't know shit. They keep the hands and the aliens segregated from the PALs." Ames immediately regretted his choice of words.

"Hate segregation," Rosie murmured. "Just hate it."

Ames struggled to cross his legs, but the bonds prevented that.

Rosie tried not to grin at the white man's consternation and terror. But he didn't kick—Beeker wanted this one operational.

"Can't leave you here," said Beeker.

"Want me to pick him up and throw him against the fence and fry him?" Marty suggested eagerly. "That way we can test the current."

Beeker shook his head. "We need this one to read the maps."

"What about the other one?" said Marty. "We don't need the other one. Can I fry him?"

"No," said Beeker. "Where's that whiskey I told you to bring along?"

Disappointed, Marty pulled a flask of J&B out of his pocket and handed it to the Cherokee.

"Not for me, Applebaum," said Beeker impatiently. "Pour it down that one's throat."

He pointed to the unconscious man on the ground.

In the morning he'd be found unconscious in the guardhouse, drunk out of his mind with a broken nose and crushed testicles and a garbled tale of what had happened to him.

Beeker had considered just killing him, but realized that was unnecessary. When Jones discovered his gatehouse was no longer manned, he'd know his security had been breached. So there was no point in actually killing the guard.

Besides, he thought, there would be enough death later on.

25

As Cowboy stood digging his ditches, he was wondering what this would have been like if the Black Berets hadn't gotten back together again. What would it have been like if Beeker hadn't insisted on all their training and all their exercises? Sure, Cowboy still sneaked his toots of coke, but they were few and far between these days.

He recalled the time he'd lived on Mother C. Suckled at the sweet bitch's breast, he thought. Cocaine was the only thing in the world he loved as much as Latin ladies. Mother C filled his life at one time, forgave his sins, obliterated his sorrows. She had also wasted his body, he realized, dragging him down to cadaver weight before Beeker stepped in and abolished her from his system, except for her occasional surreptitious visits; no longer his mother, she was a back-street floozy.

Now Cowboy knew that if he had been still living with her, he could never have survived the grueling labor that was being forced on him. His mates on the chain gang, Manuel included, went through the motions of the difficult work with a resignation that Cowboy could never have conjured up. He was getting through this because he was in tip-top shape, and because he was just making believe it was one of Beeker's little items to keep them hard and ready.

Cowboy tried to remember if there had been as much pain during Beeker's initial training as there was now. Could there have been? He recalled the endless sit-ups and push-ups, the constant running, and the horrible devil's contraption—the Universal Gym Machine.

Yes, the training had been this bad, he concluded. But it had been different because he'd been with the rest of them, men he had survived Vietnam with, men he had gotten to know better than any other humans on earth. His friends. His only real friends in his whole fucking life. The ones who'd die for him quicker than they'd light a lady's cigarette.

A weird sensation came over him, a feeling of being a little boy. He was exhausted. He was sleepy. He wanted to be saved, to be taken away from this damn place. And only his friends could do it.

So where were they? he wondered. Why weren't they here?

Of course, he suddenly realized, he would never have been here at all if it hadn't been for the Black Berets. Fuck it! Why did they have to be such hotshot assholes all the time, making believe they were fucking Marines jumping off ships to save the world? Why couldn't they just sit on the damn farm and snort coke and drink good whiskey? Because Beeker wouldn't let them, he thought, and smashed his pickax into the dry, resistant ground. Because Beeker wanted them to be the best fighting force in the world. *Thwummp!* Because Beeker had to have them ready at any moment to save motherhood and apple pie. *Thwummp!* Because Beeker had to insure that his son grew up among honorable men. *Thwummp!* Because Beeker was a fucking Marine and fucking Marines never stopped being fucking Marines and they—

"Hey, hey . . ." It was Seeley, standing behind Cowboy. "Slow down, you'll burn out."

Cowboy stood up straight and ran an arm across his forehead to catch the suddenly greater flow of sweat. He took a deep breath and went back to work, this time at the regulated, desultory pace that Manuel and the other Mexicans had set for themselves.

One step above the whip, he thought. That's how fast you worked.

And why work faster when there was no reward at the end? Not more food, not money, not a piece of ass, not even an hour's sleep extra.

"What was that about?" Manuel asked, as usual not looking directly at Cowboy, but continuing his labor.

"I was just thinking about my best friend," Cowboy replied.

Cowboy had never figured out the exact times they were chained to the beds to sleep and when they were woken up for work. Maybe it was a simple matter of dawn and dusk, he thought. Meals of cheap beans and rice, chemically treated water, hours of work, and too little time for sleep.

He did know, even after a few days, that it was too early for them to wake him now. He had gone off with the images of Beeker and the others in his mind. Dreaming, he was taking Tsali on vacation to Acapulco, where all the women were dark and willing.

Now someone was shaking his foot. He dragged himself out of his deep sleep and forced his eyes open.

It was Seeley and a couple of other men. "Come on, flyboy," Seeley said. "The big man wants to see you."

They had unlocked the ankle shackles, releasing him from bondage. Cowboy automatically reached down and massaged his skin where it had been rubbed raw by the metal. It hurt. It woke him up. Seeley gestured and Cowboy stood.

"Whew, he stinks," one of the other men said.

Quickly, before he could protest, Cowboy's hands were cuffed behind his back and he was shoved forward. Without any explanation for the strange break in routine, the guards guided him out of the barracks. At first Cowboy thought this might be some scam that Seeley had devised for his escape. But the rough treatment that he got from the others discouraged that brief hope.

They all stopped at a tap on an above-ground water line. There was a rubber hose attached. One of them turned the water on and sprayed Cowboy with the cold flow. At first it sent unexpected chills through him, but then he welcomed it. He wasn't overly fond of the four days' encrustation of dirt on his body. He probably did stink, he thought, and couldn't smell it because he'd been living in a group that stank a good deal worse.

Seeley, who'd gone away for a few minutes, returned and tossed Cowboy a bar of soap.

"Might as well do it right," Seeley said to the other two guards.

The guards let Cowboy have the soap, but to make up for the favor, they directed the harsh stream of water directly at Cowboy's crotch, and when he turned around, at the raw spot on his ankle.

Cowboy danced and howled.

Had only four days of captivity lowered his threshold of pain that much? he wondered.

The night air had dried Cowboy by the time they got to the big house. Jones was sitting on the veranda, a tall iced drink in one hand, a fat cigar in the other. He smiled at Cowboy's delivery, stark naked.

"You need a cigar," said Jones, "to keep away the stink of the Mexicans. I hear if you live with 'em, you pick it up."

"Where's Isabella?" Cowboy demanded, chains and guards and guns be damned.

"I figured you'd ask that question," said Jones easily, "so I checked up on her. She's doing fine, from what I hear. Found some work she's really good at. Though they tell me she tires out after fifteen or twenty in a row. . . ."

Cowboy said nothing. No curse. No snarl. They'd be lost on Jones, he thought. No, not lost on him. That's what Jones got fat on, the curses of people he'd trampled down. He got nothing from Cowboy.

But inside, thinking of Isabella, Cowboy's mind warped.

Jones smiled again.

". . . and after about twenty-five," he went on, "they say she starts to bleed . . ."

"You slime-hole!"

Jones smiled, and leaned back in the rocker with satisfaction. It was what he'd been waiting for.

At the same moment a guard stepped forward, one Cowboy hadn't seen before. In his hand was a long, stick-like thing. With a smile he flipped a switch with his thumb and touched the end of it to Cowboy's right thigh. There was a small yellow spark, and Cowboy felt the electric current surge through him. It was over in two seconds, but by that time, Cowboy had collapsed onto the ground, his muscles contracted in intense pain and his mind blotted of every thought except *Don't let that happen again!*

The guard moved forward and again touched the thing to Cowboy's thigh. *"No!"* Cowboy couldn't help himself. He had to protest any repetition of that agony.

"A cattle prod, Mr. Hatcher." Jones sucked on his cigar. "Mr. Sherwood Hatcher. Mr. Sherwood Hatcher of the Black Berets."

Cowboy had to look up at that. So Jones had learned who he was, and more importantly, who the team was. They had known that their reputation had grown a lot over the past year. In those few months they had run four operations, all of them spectacular successes. The underground of the world that dealt with violence, with war, with revolution, with destruction and manipulation had to have become aware of a small unit of men that would take on anyone. And that had the skills and the guts to win. In every case.

Jones knew. But how much did he know? Cowboy wondered. Enough to be scared?

"Your friends out in the fields are gonna have to get along without you, Mr. Hatcher. From now on, I'm gonna raise you up to the status of personal bodyguard."

Cowboy looked up sharply.

"That is, you're gonna protect me. So that if somebody shoots at me—like some of your friends, for instance—they're gonna have to shoot you first. But it's not gonna get to that, 'cause you're gonna be a lure too. Lure 'em out here. Then I shoot first, Mr. Hatcher. Or my boys here do. And then, when all your friends are dead and buried in their shallow graves, Mr. Hatcher, you get to go back out on the line."

"They're not coming here," said Cowboy, " 'cause they don't know where I am."

"Then they're not as smart as I've heard," said Jones. "If they don't show within the week, then I'll drop 'em a little hint. I want to meet your friends, Mr. Hatcher. I want to see their faces and judge their character and take measurements for their coffins. I had no idea that when I sent my boys over to Louisiana that they were gonna be treading so close to you and your friends."

Cowboy said nothing.

"Just as well to get the whole bunch of you out of the way. Don't want nothing to hurt my plans, Mr. Hatcher. And if there's anything I got, it's plans that don't need fucking-up by a station-wagon load of maladjusted Vietnam veterans who don't have one strain of pure white blood in five."

Cowboy was naked, cuffed, surrounded by guards. He didn't know how much Jones really knew about them. He didn't have any idea where Isabella was being kept, or really, if she was even still alive.

Seemed best on the whole not to put up a whole lot of protest, and in general, to keep his trap shut.

Just keep that damned thing off my nuts, he thought, looking askance at the cattle prod, its switch still flicked to the on position.

It was not the barracks. He could be thankful for that. It was actually a bed, and on the beds were honest-to-god sheets. He could smell the detergent that had been used to wash the sheets. Goddamn, but that sheet was *clean,* he thought. Still, it was hard to feel totally at ease, considering the chains that bound his ankles and the ropes that bound his wrists to the bedposts.

Cowboy had no idea yet just how Jones was going to use him against the Black Berets. Probably strap Cowboy to that outrageous belly like a cummerbund. Trying to neutralize the other Black Berets and leave them without the ability to fight. What would they do? he wondered.

Cowboy hoped Beeker would make the right decision. Remember the purpose of the group, who they were, and the risks that they had all chosen to accept together. Cowboy hoped Beeker would decide to let him die. That was the only decision a responsible leader could make, wasn't it? he asked himself. If they had to blow a tunnel in Cowboy's belly to get to Jones, which one of those men would hesitate to pull the trigger?

Not one of them. Not one of them would hesitate. Cowboy took a kind of grim satisfaction in that.

Then his pleasure faded away, once he'd turned the situation around. Would *he* be willing or able to do that to one of the others? Would he kill Rosie to get the group's target? Would he fire his

M16 into Beeker's gut in order to take on the assigned enemy? Or would he crumble in the face of that impossible task, that inhuman purpose?

He wondered what it would be like to face Beeker when the half-breed was holding up the rifle that would blow away his soul. It would come, that time. Cowboy was sure of it. But that certainty didn't frighten Cowboy. He just felt sorry for Billy Leaps, sorry that the guy would have to go through with that. Because he would do it—follow through. Don't raise your rifle unless you intend to fire it. Maybe a moment of hesitation—for old times' sake—but then the Cherokee would squeeze the trigger. The fucking Marine in him would do it, he thought. Well, Cowboy had saved Beeker's life a couple of times, and Beeker had saved his life as well. Because of one another, they'd had a lot more years than they should have had. Better to be shot dead by your best friend, he concluded, than to have your nuts torched by a bigoted redneck wielding the world's meanest cattle prod.

Cowboy prayed that night, in his chains, prayed to the Catholic god—Isabella and Manuel's god. Prayed that when he died, it would be Beeker who pulled the trigger.

26

When the four Black Berets heard the telephone ring they all stared at it with suspicion. It was only the cowed Ames, tied to a chair in the corner, who managed a glimmer of hope from the sound.

Beeker moved over and lifted the receiver. "Yeah."

"I gotta see you, Beeker." The voice belonged to a man. Certainly not to Delilah. Certainly not to the desk clerk. Beeker's back stiffened.

"Who's this?"

"A friend. You have to believe me. A friend."

Beeker thought for two seconds. "Got no friends in Texas."

"You better get one soon. Real soon. If you want your pal Cowboy back . . . alive."

"Where? When?"

"There's a roadhouse. Down the state highway from where you are. Go south. No troops, Beeker. Just you."

"When?"

"Ten minutes."

"You got it."

Beeker slammed down the phone and told the others what had happened.

"You can't go alone!" Rosie insisted. "We'll—"

"He found Billy Leaps, he may have already have seen us," said Harry, interrupting the black man.

"I'm gonna be outside with my M60," Marty insisted. "I'm

154

gonna waste any man who walks out of there before you tell him he can. I'm gonna—"

"You're gonna do nothing," Beeker commanded. He moved quickly, checking load in the Colt snubby under his coat, touching the knife in his belt, checking the black fiberglass Sting he kept at his ankle, just in case. "I'm going in alone. I owe Cowboy."

"We all owe Cowboy," Harry said.

"Not like I do," said Beeker.

An ambush can be set up in an ancient Hindu temple; it can just as easily occur at a fundamentalist's tent-revival meeting. In the Jerusalem marketplace cantaloupes sometimes explode. In London's Regent Park grenades are sometimes launched out of staid black perambulators. The enemy may wear the robes of a monk, or she may be masked in clown-white and amuse children on the street corner a few moments before she slits the throat of an arriving dignitary. Children alone in airports are not always in search of their parents, and old women in East European pastry shops can sometimes cut a man's life very short. Beeker had seen all these things and more. So he wasn't about to discount the danger involved in standing at the bar of the Saddleback Grill.

The music was Waylon Jennings. The beer was Lone Star. The smell was a mixture of sweat and dust and lost dreams. There were a million dives just like it in Texas, in the southwest, and in America. Working-class men downing cheap beer, listening to country-and-western music that told them true love and money were things you could get if only you looked for them hard enough.

Beeker looked around. He was a half-breed and would never be mistaken for anything else—not the sort generally welcomed at the Saddleback. He just assumed that the fact he looked sober kept the drunken rednecks off his back. Soberness, six feet of muscle, and a military bearing straight off a recruiting poster did the job.

When one man did dare to move close to him at the bar, Beeker looked at him and was startled, just for a minute. This could be an ambush. This could be his enemy. It wouldn't be the first time the enemy had a familiar face. Not by a long shot.

The man ordered a Lone Star. Beeker looked more closely.

155

Somehow it had to have been in 'Nam. But where? he wondered. When? He couldn't remember that. There had been so many.

"They got your friend," Seeley said.

Beeker shrugged.

Seeley took a deep breath. "You know who Jones is?"

Beeker nodded, but still didn't speak.

"The flyer is Jones's shield—against you and your buddies. If Jones can't kill you—and he's gonna give it a good try, anyway—then he's at least gonna keep you busy till he gets his operation going good. Then you and your friends don't matter so much—not once things get going. You got any idea what I'm talking about? 'Cause I'm not gonna spell things out. You got to already know."

"I know," said Beeker. "What I don't know is, why are you telling me this?"

"I owe you, half-breed. I don't like owing any man. But I do owe you."

"What for?" Beeker pursued.

"If you don't remember right now, you will later. That's good enough. It was 'Nam, but I figure you know that. That would have been the easy part to figure out. Guys like you, you got the 'Nam, and you got about fuck-all else in your life."

Beeker thought: *A year ago that would've been true.* But not now. Not with the resurrected team, five dead men pulled up out of limbo on a frayed rope.

"You need me," Seeley broke into Billy Leaps's thoughts.

"Need *you?*"

"You haven't got your flyer. He's the one you're supposed to rescue. I know that. I can fly. I can fly anything. I'll take you."

Beeker's eyes half-closed. "Why the fuck am I going to trust you with my team?"

"Because I owe you, I told you that. Because I was a jarhead. You trust that. Because I was in 'Nam. That means something. And most of all because I know where your flyboy is. Precisely where he is.

"I got maps of the layout." It might have been showing too much of his hand, but the captured Ames had been able to sketch

156

out the ranch's headquarters. "I got another flyer." Applebaum could do it, he thought.

"But you don't have a flyer as good as me. And you can't afford to use one of your men on anything but the attack. Just guessing, but I'm right, ain't I? You got nothing to spare if you go up against Jones, do you?"

"How are we ever going to go anywhere with this fucker?" Rosie was looking at a piece of war surplus. A big piece of war surplus. It was a CH-53. A Jolly Green Giant, a piece of military hardware designed for the transport of goods, not soldiers. It was intended for the transferring hardware, not fighting men. What if those assholes had Cobras like Cowboy's? he wondered. This species of flying boxcar wouldn't do shit against them. God*damn*.

Beeker, Seeley, and the present owner of the 'copter were deep in conversation. Beeker was nodding his head too often for Rosie. Much too often. And then he dug into his pocket and brought out a big manila envelope, the one he'd stuffed with hundred-dollar bills. "God*damn*," Rosie swore. The fucker had gone and bought it.

The truth was, Rosie didn't care about the aircraft. It could have been anything so far as he was concerned. It could have been one of those new special things that they had bought for Cowboy. Damn, Rosie thought, Cowboy could fly my mama with a pair of water wings and an eggbeater and that would be okay with me. Really it would have. He trusted Cowboy that much. But this? Hell, a fucked-up piece of military surplus and a fucked-up strange-as-hell pilot they were supposed to trust with their lives?

"God*damn!*"

The 'copter had been moved up to the end of the runway, into an empty hangar. While Rosie fumed and Harry looked on stoically, Marty was getting excited. "Sure, we can do it, sure." He ran his hand along the side of the fuselage. "No problem."

Marty went over to the pilot and they began to talk excitedly. The man who had sold them the 'copter was agreeing to something else. Beeker was waiting.

They worked through the night. With Marty and Seeley giving the instructions, they used the welding tools and all the other equipment they had been loaned. "No sweat," Marty kept saying. "God*damn,*" Rosie always responded, but assisted when he was able.

No one doubted that they were going to go on this mission. They had to. One of them had been captured, one of them had to be rescued. It was their code, the one thing that mattered above all others. They could not abandon a Black Beret. The idea was never even mentioned as a possibility. It never would be.

By the time dawn had lighted up the open doors of the hangar and wakened Rosie and Harry, napping contentedly on the cement floor without cushions for their heads, the 'copter was ready. Its cargo doors had been removed. Instead there were just wide openings, just like the Hueys in 'Nam. Openings for the mounting of guns. Openings for men to jump to the ground, their rifles ready, their prayers begging only that Charlie not be totally prepared for the onslaught.

The lettering on the side of the craft had been painted over at the request of the owner, and in the midst of the installation of the M60's, Marty had found time to spray paint the legend I BRING DEATH with a crude skull beneath. The skull had Marty's own grin.

Marty was still working feverishly in the open cargo bays as Beeker sketched out the mission plan.

"We're rappelling in," he said.

That stopped them all.

Harry and Rosie exchanged glances.

Rappelling in with a pilot none of them had ever flown with before?

It was one thing to dangle defenselessly beneath a chopper with Cowboy at the controls but a pilot they weren't even sure was on their side?

"No other way to do it," said Beeker. "I've gone over these maps a million times."

Beeker had tested Ames and Seeley, making each man separately mark the locations inside the ranch. It was still possible this was a set-up, that the two men had orders to mislead any enemy if captured, that Jones had actually gone so far as to plant a set of false ranch plans in the brains of every one of his guards and merc employees. But that was unlikely, and Beeker had to chance it. The two men had agreed on every important point. Their recollection of schedules and locations had been nearly identical. Their minor disagreements were most easily ascribed to faulty assumptions or bad observation.

Jones's set-up fed on paranoia, traded on paranoia, and it instilled paranoia in others. Jones and his group were just the types to spend a quarter of their time and resources planning against the unplannable. But Beeker didn't have time to try to second-guess Jones, nor was he the kind of leader who hangs fire until all the plans are final and complete and foolproof. He knew that plans in war are never foolproof—they may have to change, minute by minute. At some point, while he must be careful of his troops' welfare, a leader has to commit himself and them to action. Beeker had decided that this was one of those times: he would have to go on the best information available.

He had the men, well armed. He had secured transport. He knew the location of the enemy. He had planned for those contingencies he could. This was it. Time to move.

"But this bastard!" Rosie pointed to Seeley. "You know damn well how dangerous rappelling is. You got a pilot doesn't know what he's doing, you can be gone. We ain't even seen this guy's résumé—we don't even know which fucking side he's on—and you want us to trust him with our goddamn *lives?*"

"What I want," said Beeker, tugging on one of the newly installed rings on which their lives would depend, "is for you to get Cowboy out of there."

27

Oh, the *whoop-whoop-whoop!* That sound, that deadly sound, was like so many of the things in 'Nam. Something that a man thought could only exist there. What son of Rosie's mother should have to listen to that ungodly sound here in the United States? Rosie asked himself. The announcement of invasion, the forces coming so swiftly that the enemy couldn't even take advantage of the noisy warning.

The 'copter was moving at over 100 knots an hour above the Texas prairie. Rosie and Marty were holding on to the grips of the M60's that hung out the door. The wind blew hard at their faces. Rosie felt the strong breeze whip his clothes and sweep his newly shaved head.

Where are the jungles? Rosie wanted to know. When you're up in a 'copter and holding on to an M60 you should have jungles beneath you. He knew that. Because Rosie had stood just like this countless times before, with the wind, the fear of the coming battle, the lust for the action, all of it consuming him.

But always with jungle below.

The brown of Texas seemed so incongruous to him, so strange a sight. As though all the bombers in 'Nam had finally had the leisure to do their work right, spraying their Agent Orange in quantities sufficient to complete defoliation. There was hardly any vegetation left, and certainly no jungle. It made Rosie queasy. But all he had to do was grip harder on his rifle and he knew this wasn't a dream. Uh-unh, this was the real thing. Someone puts that kind of muscle between your hands and it is the *real thing*.

All their instructions ran back through Rosie's head. There were guards in the main house at all times, but they usually carried only sidearms. No big deal. There was a barracks full of the off-duty ones a few hundred feet from the house. That was target one for Marty. Rosie looked over at the LAWs the little wild man had brought along. This was one time Rosie was not sorry that Marty had gone hogwild with his blow-'em-ups.

The barracks would be full of the hard-core security guards. The ones that the Great White Leader, D. Jerrold Jones, had hand-picked. Hard men, most of them seasoned mercs, they were as dangerous as they came. They had to be eliminated.

The 'copter moved quickly. The sound carried ahead of it. Rosie could see the small figures at first standing still and probably trying to locate the sound and then, on some command, running like hell. Like Satan himself when he sees Jesus coming, Rosie thought. Jesus in the air, with sworded angels in cammie.

It was the same way that Rosie would have run if he heard incoming 'copters while he was in a base. Sure would run like that, he thought. Except *faster*.

The 'copter moved in. Marty had sworn that he'd take the LAWs to their furthest limits. Well, if anyone could, sure as hell was going to be Marty. When the stakes were biggest, that's when Marty took his biggest chances.

Always paid off.

So far.

Screaming with delirious joy, Marty handled the big machine as though it was a piece of plastic. Some plastic, Rosie thought as the deadly mechanisms fired Marty's toys down to the ground. It only took seconds for the familiar explosions to sound.

One, two . . . three . . . four, five.

Marty always gave them a rhythm. Like a signature.

The 'copter veered and Rosie got to see the destruction. Holy shit. God*damn*! Applebaum had done it! he thought. The flames roared up from what had been, ten seconds before, the mercs' barracks. There were little stick figures running all around it. Rosie knew them. They were the enemy, the enemy that always had to be gotten. How strange they looked from this distance.

Rosie wondered if it had always been so easy for the airboys, to stay way up here and look way down there and never have to see the agony on the face of a dying man, a man whose last meal probably hadn't been all that special—because he had no intention of being dead within the next few hours. Pull triggers, shift levers, punch the buttons that spasmed the computers. You never had to hear the screams. You never had to see the suffering. Jittering stick figures just didn't pull enough psychic weight to make it into nightmares a decade or two along the line.

But stick figures or not, Rosie could look down and he knew what was really happening. He knew that that one little Tinkertoy running faster than all the others with a trail of fire behind him was actually in flames himself. The Tinkertoys chasing him were trying to put out the fire. They just wanted to help. But the shocked pain of the burning man was too much, he was too panicked and, as such men do, he thought he could outrun the flames, outrun the death that was sure to come.

Rosie only wished that one of his friends would shoot him dead. When the fire got a man that bad, there wasn't no use. There was just the agony of it. If he'd had a chance, Rosie would have done the man a favor, and that's what it would have been. Made no difference about friends or foes there, he thought, a man should have a quick death when he was that far gone.

But Rosie didn't get the chance to do his good deed for the day. The 'copter was on the move again. Fast and sure, deadly and accurate, Seeley hadn't fucked them over yet, at any rate. Marty was launching again, shooting into the supply depot, the place where the arms and fuel for this little army were cached. He was yelling something joyfully again, but Rosie couldn't hear it over the rotaries and didn't even try. Marty's joy was almost incoherent anyway.

BAAAAAAAMMMMM!

An explosion sounded through the 'copter, shaking it, jarring Rosie out of his crawl and onto his side. The pilot veered quickly, too quickly almost, to get out of the way of whatever it was. Rosie nearly rolled out the bay. He caught himself the last second.

Missiles from the ground was Rosie's first thought. Then he saw Marty's grin, and he looked out.

A mushroom cloud.

Goddamn, he thought, the little blond fuck had finally pulled it on them.

Goddamn, Billy Leaps had told him no nukes.

Goddamn, where'd he get hold of it?

But then Rosie realized that the mushroom cloud wasn't nuclear. Because if it had been Rosie wouldn't have been standing there staring at it and cursing Applebaum. Rosie would have been a little puff of white smoke lost in a big puff of gray smoke.

Marty had scored a direct hit on Jones's fuel depot.

The building went in a mushroom cloud, and all around it were smaller puffs of orange and red flames—smaller reserves and gas tanks that had heated to the point of ignition.

"I'm fucking wonderful," Marty boasted.

"You're fucking sick," Rosie said, and wished he was farther away. But once again he was glad that Martin Applebaum was on his side.

It had taken, tops, two minutes for Marty to destroy half the camp below. From the size and fury of the conflagrations below, rising impossibly high from the desert itself it seemed, the job had been the same complete destruction that Marty was noted for. Seeley glanced over his shoulder once at Marty, puzzled and fearful.

But now came the hard part, Rosie knew. The enemy was alerted, and even if he was half-assed, he was awake and ready. At least those of the enemy left alive.

Rosie gripped his M60 and watched as they grouped themselves below. Big heroes! he thought. Dumb fucks was more like it. They were going to try to take down the helicopter with their rifles. But the Berets had presents for them. Lots and lots of little surprises, spilled out of the narrow mouths of the chopper's Gatlings.

The little stick figures started to fall, the unlucky ones. Then the smart ones got their asses out of the way. The ones that ran away from the house were smart, anyway. Harry and Marty weren't too interested in them. They were concerned with securing the LZ, the landing zone where the Black Berets would descend. That meant that the enemy had to be kept away from the big mansion. Any one of them that moved in that mistaken direction got it. A good-night kiss of steel.

The figures that had moved in the wrong direction were down for the count. Rosie could rest up. Rest up and get ready for the big one, he thought. He knew that from this point on he was going to see the faces of the men he killed.

28

Four of them at once. The maximum in the best of times. But this wasn't the best of times and they didn't know shit about the pilot they were trusting. But they went through with it. They went through with it as though they had been doing it every day of their lives for a year.

Each rope was tied to three rings in the floor of the helicopter. For the umpteenth time in his life Rosie was trusting Beeker and Applebaum to have done their jobs. Were the rings in solid? Were the knots really secure? If they weren't Rosie might just as well jump out the open doorway now and save himself a handful of friction burns. He'd die if those knots weren't going to hold his weight. Rosie put the midpoint of the sling rope he'd been given over his left hip. He made a full turn around the waist, so that the running ends dangled before him. Then he put them through his legs and tied the rope off over his left hip. The square knot came right back to him and so did the two half hitches.

The snap link went over the X at the front of his body so that the gate closed up and out. Now he was ready, and so was everything else, apparently. The rope dangled down from the 'copter, its end a few feet over the roof of what Rosie thought of as the silly-looking fake plantation house. As soon as his rope touched the roof . . .

Now!

He moved out. Clutching the rope, he stepped onto the skid, then lowered himself as quickly as possible. He had made only a couple of turns of the rope around the snap link. This wasn't a carnival ride to be drawn out as long as possible. No way! He wanted out of the sky as fast as he could have it.

How often had he seen this done in 'Nam? How often had the results been disastrous? Men dangled from ropes that didn't reach the ground because an incompetent pilot lifted up a bit too much. Men were left slowly swinging targets for the marksmanship practice of chuckling Charlie. Or the assholes had fucked up their own ropes. Fucked them up so badly that there was no way the rope wasn't going to tangle and leave them like a big green knot in the rope, halfway down to the ground. Big green knot that was going to bleed like a son-of-a-bitch when it got shot full of Charlie's bullets.

Rappelling was the means of last resort. You put all your men there, right up in the air, the 'copter having given the enemy warning, and you pray that your men and your pilot are good enough that the right ones get down to the ground.

The reason for the risk?

Because then your men are just where you want them. Delivered on a dime. No land movements, no exposed runways, nothing. Troops on the spot. Just like the Black Berets right now.

Going down the rope, Rosie felt in another world. He wasn't thinking about the 'copter above, or the steeply pitched roof below, or two dozen men with rifles surrounding the house and taking aim, or the other three guys going down their own ropes a few feet away—just the ropes, his own hands guiding his descent, and the snap link that, so far, was working just right. That's all Rosie was thinking about. Nothing else.

Then he was on the roof. Bounced like he had just been delivered by the stork. His hands on fire from the burns. But alive and safe.

Out of the rope.

And down. Down flat because there were bullets. They whizzed above his head, and they splintered the shiny wooden gutters at the edge of the roof.

Above him the 'copter veered away.

Seeley, that fucker, had done it right, Rosie thought. Goddamn, Rosie would have to figure out something about that one later.

Rosie, not even daring to raise his arm, slid his M16 along the roof slates until it came into position in front of him. They had already taken care of at least a hundred men in these attacks. At least a hundred. You'd think the rest would just understand that when four men off one hundred, he thought, the odds had very little to do with actual numbers, but reckoned as skill against skill. But the message hadn't been received.

Stretching out on the steeply inclined slate roof, so that he seemed in danger every moment of simply sliding down and pitching out over the ground, Rosie took aim.

He could see about a dozen men down below, stupidly using a line of three pick-up trucks as cover. Damn, they were making this too easy.

Rosie figured the drop to the trucks and he dropped a fat, high-explosive round into the breech on the M203 that rode under the barrel of his M16. Let's see, he mused; the gas tank is right—

WHOOOOOSH!

There went the first one, orange flames and screams.

One more quick round from the M203 and—

WHOOOOOSH!

Reddish flames and screams.

WHOOOOOSH!

Reddish flames and a third set of screams.

Now why, Rosie wondered, did two of the trucks explode in reddish flames, and the first one in orange flames? Marty would know. Rosie made a mental note to ask him later.

The men behind the trucks who hadn't died in the explosions were on fire. And wouldn't you know, Rosie thought, that asshole D. Jerrold Jones had given his men polyester uniforms. And they burned like polyester—hot and melting and impossible to quench. Good old one-hundred-percent Texas cotton wouldn't burn like that, Rosie reflected as he picked off the frantic human torches one by one. His good deed for the day—alleviating a whole lot of polyester misery.

With the last one down that he could see, Rosie had a free moment. He turned and sighted the rest of the Black Beret crew. As agreed, each had taken a corner of the house. The combined effect of their rifles had been to disperse any planned assault on the building. The fires from the storage depot and the barracks had removed all close cover. After Rosie's show, no one else was going to be stupid enough to try to hide behind one of the few remaining vehicles. It was, Rosie figured, a species of luck that there was no egress from the house onto the roof. He wondered what they were thinking in the rooms below.

He wondered which window D. Jerrold Jones was looking out of.

That was the next objective. The house itself. Where Cowboy was.

Rosie crawled down to the gutter and leaned over. There was a window there. If he could do a flip over the edge and land right, just right, he could go in feet first. If he went too far, he'd fall three stories onto the concrete pool patio and no more Rosie. That, or he could do the easy thing and try that balcony over there. But, of course, anyone with a brain downstairs was going to be standing right inside those French doors, with a rifle pointing out.

Marty's intense screaming punctuated the barrage that continued from the other three corners of the building's roof. Rosie looked over and saw the little runt with his M60. How did that skinny child ever carry that thing, he wondered, especially from the air, especially rappelling? Well, if that asshole could do that, then Rosie could do this.

He gripped harder. He tensed his legs. One hand, that's all he could use if he was going to hold onto the M16. Rosie had no intention of going anywhere in that house without the rifle. One hand attached to one arm trained by William Leaps Beeker, USMC-retired. Okay, Beak, Rosie thought, let's see what you've done for this one arm. And damn you if it don't work.

Rosie hefted himself and felt his body flying through thin air. Flipping over in a swing that seemed curiously slow and leisurely. And then a moment when he stopped, his feet pressing against a flat surface.

Glass.

Shards of glass slid all up around him, slicing his skin—but he

168

was through and into the room, rather than sliding down the walls of the habitation of D. Jerrold Jones.

He even landed on his feet. Goddamn, thank you, Billy Leaps, he thought. If I ever get out of this I'll join the goddamn circus. And then he realized that he was even in battle stance, with his rifle pointed at the one person who was already in the room, ready to fire, fire right at—

Isabella Cifuentes.

Looking a little worn, a little frightened, but putting on a brave smile all the same.

29

Beeker was only able to use hand signals to confirm his instructions to Harry and Marty. They had outlined the options and now he had to trust them to know which one he'd decided to take.

Harry followed his lead. He and Beeker had brought extra rope with them. They quickly secured them to one of the many chimneys that stuck up through the roof. Marty didn't leave off his fire for a moment. That was the plan. But Rosie should have been helping him, and where was Rosie?

There was no time to find out. They had to move. Marty would stay at his post, his M60 denying admittance to the building by anyone. The rope was secure. Using the mountain climbing techniques that they had all practiced, and the ropes they'd brought along, Beeker and Harry rappelled down the side of the building, avoiding the windows as best they could. They didn't want to be observed at all—this part of the visit was still unexpected.

At the ground they ducked under the windows, unseen by a couple of men who had rifle barrels sticking through the broken glass. The poorly trained guards were stupidly looking for an assault from the ground to accompany the airborne attack.

Only when they got to the glass doors that Seeley had promised them led to the series of main rooms on the first floor did Harry and Beeker stand, their M16's ready. A nod from Beeker, a prayer to each of their gods that Cowboy wasn't going to be inside the room, and in they went.

The glass smashed open. They stalked slowly forward with automatic rounds of the M16's spitting. As they sent shotgunlike waves of bullets into the room, plaster, glass, fabric, and wood all exploded around them.

All those things and some flesh and blood as well.

There had been three guards with the assignment to stand sentinel there. The first one had his life eliminated with the opening salvo. His face had melted away into a sagging, melancholy mask of blood and white bone.

The second tried to get a couple of shots off, but Harry had seen him first. Harry's M16 got him in the shoulder. The power of the automatic fire spun him around. His own bullets sputtered uselessly into the ceiling.

The third had tried too. But Beeker didn't need the extra shots Harry did. Two bullets to the forehead. And there were no shots in return.

"Through the hallway," Seeley had said. Ames had confirmed.

The marble-tiled floor gleamed white and black. Beeker and Harry moved over the cool, polished surface. They turned a corner. There, waiting for them, but also somehow surprised to find them there, was the last line of defense.

Seven guards. Two of them with only handguns. The other five with rifles. Seven guards who glanced at one another, and waited for their leader to tell them what to do, and their leader wondering if he should say *Capture* or *Shoot* or call for Jones or what.

But Harry and Beeker didn't need to discuss their strategy, and Beeker's orders in this situation had long ago been implanted in Harry's mind. They both knew what to do.

Shoot.

And they both knew when to do it.

Now.

Harry was on the right, so he took out that end.

Harry went for the chest. Always the chest. If you hit a man anywhere in that area the force of the M16's bullets would spin him, knock him off balance, make him miss his mark.

Beeker on the left, and he took care of those.

Beeker shot quicker and cleaner. The forehead, and behind the forehead, the brain.

"Fire," shouted the leader of Jones's hallway guards, but by then all his men were dead—and by the time he realized that, so was he.

Seven guards had managed to fire about half a dozen shots. Plugging the wallpaper. Smashing the marble flooring. Shattering a vase on a hall table, and splashing Harry with the water that had been inside it.

Harry and Beeker moved down the corridor, to a pair of enormous oak doors at the end, with carved panels and brass handles.

Harry stood out of the way, his rifle raised.

Beeker lifted his steel-toed boot and kicked straight out. The heavy wood splintered, and the doors sagged open.

Beeker and Harry were out of the way of the barrage of bullets—that did not come.

"Welcome to my home, gentlemen."

They looked inside. A magnificent mahogany study. Carved paneling. Antique desk and furniture. Oriental carpets. Stone hearth. Stained glass windows. D. Jerrold Jones in a leather chair behind the enormous desk.

The only incongruous note was a tiny folding metal chair next to Jones, and tied to the chair, Sherwood Hatcher, naked, with the naked barrel of a pistol pressed to his temple.

Beeker and Harry stood silent in the doorway.

"I'm gonna kill him," said Jones, "if your arms aren't on the floor by the time I count to five."

Discipline and loyalty did battle in Beeker's mind. He glanced around the room. Only one real exit besides the windows—a door that apparently led to another part of the house. There was Marty on the roof and Rosie somewhere else. Maybe even dead.

"One."

Beeker could get off one shot and pray it was quick and accurate enough to knock the pistol out of Jones's hand. How fast were the reflexes of a fat man? he wondered.

"Two."

Beeker knew Harry wouldn't do it. He shouldn't. This was the job of the team marksman. That was him. He was the one who had to decide if he could pull it off.

"Three."

172

If he didn't, he thought, Cowboy would be dead. The man who had been his best friend in 'Nam, the man who had saved his life six, maybe seven times. Cowboy would be dead because he hadn't put down his rifle—or because he didn't fire quickly enough.

"Four."

If he could make a show of starting to put down his rifle in the second or so that remained, Beeker thought, maybe Jones's attention would be distracted just enough so that Harry could get off a shot. If Harry realized that that was what he was supposed to do. But Harry would know that, wouldn't he? If it actually looked as if Beeker were about to give in to the fat man, if—

"Fi—"

Crack.

That's what Beeker had done. Made a feint of putting down his rifle on the count of four.

But it wasn't Harry who had fired.

It was Rosie, now grinning from the open side door.

And Jones was slumped in his chair, with most of the left side of his head gone, sprayed back into the dark cavity of the stone hearth. The enormous weight of the corpse slowly slid down to the floor, and disappeared into the well of the desk.

After that it was a mop-up operation. Seeley landed the helicopter and joined the Black Berets. He guided them around but—somewhat to Marty's disappointment—there were no more deaths. The PALs that remained alive had cleared out by the time the Black Berets got around to looking for them. The Mexicans were liberated, and let into the kitchens that had supported the mercenaries in considerable gastronomical comfort. Standing before them, Cowboy assured the aliens that if they remained for a few days—without having to do any more work, of course—they would be paid for the work that they had done.

Billy Leaps felt that he could afford to promise at least this much to the workers, considering the enormous cash payroll that Isabella found in a safe in Jones's office; Marty at least had the pleasure of blowing it open.

The Black Berets got off the ranch as quickly as they could. No point in being found all together at the scene of such carnage. Beeker just called up Delilah, and told her to get to it. That was just the sort of thing that she and her people were good at. Quiet clean-ups.

To Cowboy's chagrin, Isabella decided to remain behind at the Triple-Bar-D. With Jones's massive corpse still bleeding beneath the desk, she set out on a systematic study of the records of Ranger Petroleum that she found in the study files.

"Blondie," she said sternly, "this is the chance of a lifetime for me. Please let me have a few hours in here. You are safe, and I am safe, and I will give you a call."

That was all he could get out of her—that and a promise that she would find Manuel a good job with Mexotex, and that she would look after the boy personally. Walking away, shaking his head, Cowboy decided that there was more to this business of romance and Latin ladies than he had suspected all these years.

That evening, waiting to hear from Delilah, the Black Berets returned to the Saddleback Grill. As he always did after narrowly escaping death—he could still smell the metal of that pistol that had been pressed against his temple—Cowboy *guzzled* bourbon. Until he could grin, thinking about what he'd gone through.

Rosie poured for Cowboy, and nearly kept up.

Marty sat in a booth with Harry and told Harry everything that had happened that day, even though Harry had been there and had taken part in it. When Marty had finished his story on the day's assault on the Triple-Bar-D, he began it again. Only the second time, he was in on the kill in Jones's study.

In a corner of the bar, at a small table, Billy Leaps sat with Seeley, who hadn't betrayed him after all.

The flyer pulled on his beer. "It was in 'Nam, like I told you. I was a jarhead. You know that too. I was a 'copter jockey like your buddy over there." Seeley laughed. "And he wasn't none too pleased, was he, when he found out I rappelled you guys in today?"

That was right. Cowboy hadn't liked it one little bit. He wouldn't have liked it if Marty had done it. But a fucking *stranger*?

"I was green when you met me, Beeker. Real green." Seeley's smile went away like it was never going to come back. "I dropped a load of grunts in a fire zone. Big bad me. I was scared shitless. I was fucking terrified."

Beeker said nothing. He didn't have to. Everybody in that war was terrified, he thought. Every fucking minute.

"I was supposed to go back into the LZ to pick up wounded. You were behind the lines and you were desperate to get into the action. You got on my 'copter. And I wouldn't land it. Every goddamn regulation in the book said I didn't have to. Every single one. Too many Charlies. Too much fire. The LZ wasn't secure. I was ready to turn back and then you put your sights down on the wounded there. The kids, grunts like me, that were spread out and ready to get out of there."

Beeker still didn't remember. How much had he gone through out there, how many days of hell had accumulated so that he couldn't remember a particular one anymore?

"I said no way. You said yes. I started to move in the other direction and you put your fucking service revolver against my head and told me we were both going to die before you let those jarheads go to Charlie. Found out later you pulled that shit all over 'Nam. Big hero. I landed that bird. Still don't know how. We got those kids in, and we got those kids out. I got a bronze star. I got to be a fucking hero. Because you put a gun to me and made me do it. And from then on, Beeker, I was caught. 'Cause every time something like that came up, I was sitting there, pissing my pants and thinking, *fucker's got a gun to my head* . . . and I went in there and I did what had to be done. You turned me into a Marine, Beeker. And you turned me into a pro. Two things I got to thank you for. You fucker. A Marine and a pro for life. The two things in this whole goddamn life I never wanted to happen. Not really. 'Cause look where it got me—beating fucking wetbacks to death in the fucking desert. Man, I could have sold insurance!"

Seeley stood up and threw a couple of bucks on the table. "For my beer. I don't want to owe you nothing else. Next time I see you, Beeker, remember I don't owe you shit. Remember that—'cause next time I suspect I'm going to be on the other side."

Billy Leaps watched the man walk out the door. He'd changed that man's life, and didn't remember a bit of it. Not a bit. How many others had there been? Had he done it to these four others in the Saddleback? To Harry and Rosie and Cowboy and Marty?

Was he doing it to Tsali? To his own son?

Dolly Parton was singing on the juke, and Billy Leaps listened to the words. They didn't help. And, he suspected, nothing else would either.